THE DANCE
OF DEATH

JOE CALDERWOOD

THE DANCE OF
DEATH

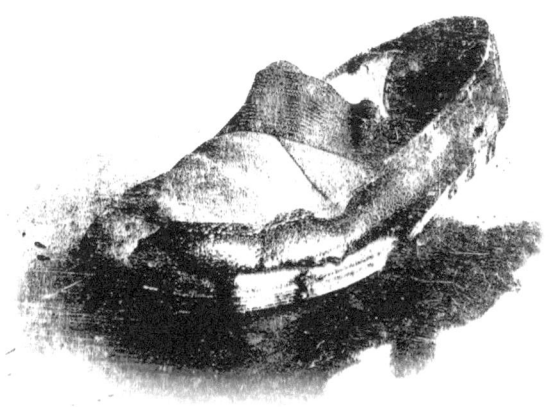

ANYONE CAN BE A KILLER. THEY JUST NEED A GOOD REASON.

Designer Credits
Cover art by **thecovercollection.com**

Interior design by **Anna Zubrytska**

Produced in the USA
Print 978-1-62134-434-6
E-Pub 978-1-62134-436-0
Mobi 978-1-62134-435-3

Published by Water Street Press
Healdsburg, California

For Gil Calderwood, thirty-nine years my partner and spouse.

CONTENTS

THE DANCE OF DEATH

Tlaxco, 1986

A lvaro Moreno, Jr. was nine years old when his father allowed him to enter a ring with a live bull for the first time. The bull was just four months old, a little less than three hundred pounds, on the small side and without the temperament to be a true fighter. So Alvaro's father told his mother.

Mrs. Moreno stood with the other spectators in the dust outside the wire field fence, the hem of her floral-patterned cotton dress fluttering in the slight breeze, her hands resting on the shoulders of Oscar, Alvaro's younger brother, who looked on, jealous, as their father led Alvaro through the cattle panel. "*No me gusta esto,*" she muttered, and the seamstress had nodded and scooped up her own small son from where he had in any case been playing too close to the gap at the bottom of the field fence, tightening her grip on him as she held him in her arms. The manager and the trainer, however, had cheered, and neither Alvaro nor his father gave any indication they'd heard Mrs. Moreno speak.

Alvaro Moreno, Sr. was a matador, a famous one. His family lived well on what he earned from his time in the ring with the bulls, and it was his wish to pass the tradition to his sons. That his sons, too, would fight bulls and make good livings, though economic considerations were not all that fueled by his hopes. Alvaro Moreno, Sr. was a romantic. Courage, he believed, was the finest trait a man could possess. "A bullfight is not a battle between a man and an animal," he told his elder son as they stood before the baby bull. "It is a fight between a man and his fears."

And Alvaro, the son, had been quite afraid.

He was glad of it.

He wanted to face his fears. The bulls, after all, were what they had come to Tlaxco to see.

They had traveled by caravan, in two cars, from Merida. Alvaro, Jr. and his little brother had ridden in the backseat of the Moreno's brand new, 1986 black Mercedes sedan, his mother in the front seat with his father at the wheel. The second car, another from the Moreno fleet, a battered but reliable olive-green Ford LTD with a sun-bleached roof, followed the Mercedes, Alvaro, Sr.'s manager at the wheel and his trainer riding shotgun. In the backseat rode the manager's wife and his three-year-old son, Jorge.

Both Moreno boys knew their father was annoyed that Jorge had been brought along on the trip, but the *abuela* who had been supposed to care for the child had taken sick. Alvaro, Sr. had told his manager to leave his wife behind in this case, but Mrs. Moreno had said no. The wife was also a seamstress, and there were costumes to be made for the new season, fittings that had to be done and, besides, the woman had been promised this small vacation. Alvaro, Sr. did not like to appear to break a promise, not to his wife, so now Jorge slept, sweating and fitful, against his mother's leg while she finished embroidering an eagle in gold thread onto the red satin collar of a new cape, her fingers efficient in spite of the bumpy journey, the many potholes in the road and her husband's necessary attempts to keep up with the car in front of them.

Alvaro, Sr. liked to drive. He liked to play a little game with his manager, laughing as he pressed the gas and pulled far ahead of the old car following him. Waiting until the LTD was out of sight before he slowed again, chuckling until he saw it again in the rearview mirror. The seamstress prayed while she stitched, that Alvaro, Sr. would soon grow tired and the trainer would be pressed to take the wheel of the Mercedes so the boss could rest. It would take nearly twenty-four hours of driving, two nights in hotels, to reach the ranch where, Alvaro, Sr. said, the finest Cabrera bulls in all of Mexico were bred.

In the Mercedes, young Alvaro and Oscar laughed while the seamstress prayed, and they urged their father to once again speed ahead. It was a great game, to kneel on their seat, look out the back window, and wait for the old Ford to appear in the cloud of dust their father raised behind them. They giggled, as children do, until the Ford emerged from the cloud, and then they begged their father to race once more. "*No me gusta esto*," Mrs. Moreno whispered her refrain to deaf ears.

They had arrived at the ranchera late in the afternoon that first day. Mrs. Moreno and the seamstress were taken by the rancher's wife to their rooms, to refresh themselves. The men followed the rancher himself out to the corrals, where hands were separating the new calves and branding them – hard, dirty work not fit for women, or for children. The three boys were herded into the kitchen to sit at a table with the rancher's two youngest sons and his many daughters. The children were all younger than Alvaro, Jr. so, while the kitchen was majestic, and the food the children were served at their long table delicious, Alvaro was bored, and a little ashamed he had not been invited to accompany the men. The children were being served a fried chicken dinner and when, at the cook's instruction, Alvaro washed his hands in the kitchen sink, he was pleased to see the heads of the birds they were being served in the drain. He picked one up in his hands and used it to tease the other children, and terrify little Jorge, which revived his spirts a little.

On the morning of the second day, early in the day while it was still cool and the sky was still steel gray, while the roosters were still crowing, the whole party accompanied the rancher to the corrals to inspect the bulls.

"You see?" Alvaro, Sr., said to his sons. "You see their fine heads, and their small hooves, and their well-proportioned horns? These things are what the Cabrera bulls are known for – these things and their bravery, and swiftness." He tousled his elder son's hair just as one of the bulls took notice of the party gathered at his fence, and the bull stepped forward, his head held high, his eyes steady on Alvaro, Sr. "Cabrera bulls," he said, his eyes locked on the glinting ones of the animal, his hand resting on his son's head, "are known for their nobility."

Alvaro did not wince at his father's touch, though it angered him, to be treated like a child. Like a child, and in front of the whole company – his mother, his father's manager and his trainer, the rancher and his hands. The other children. He did not wince, but he stepped back, which made his father laugh.

"Ho, Alvaro! You are frightened of the bull!"

"I am not!" Alvaro, Jr. protested, but too late. The party was all laughing now. "I am not!" Alvaro screamed at them.

"Come!" Alvaro, Sr. shouted, silencing his son.

Alvaro, Jr. followed his father around the barn, to another, smaller corral where the recently separated calves milled in the soft dirt. The party followed father and son, and arranged themselves behind.

"That one," Alvaro, Sr. said, waving a hand, and two of the ranch hands moved quickly to separate the selected calf from the rest of the herd and move him into a smaller, solitary pen.

"Alvaro," Mrs. Moreno whispered.

"The boy must not be afraid," Alvaro, Sr. shouted in reply.

"*No me gusta esto!*" she insisted as Alvaro, Sr. pushed his son through the cattle gate.

Inside the pen with the calf, even with his father's hand on his back, Alvaro stood as still as death. Nothing had ever looked bigger to him than the glistening red-brown calf. Nothing had ever felt more filled with danger than the calf's dark eyes upon him. Nothing had ever felt as silent as the quiet that fell over the party as they watched the boy and the young bull. He felt fear tickle his muscles, and he wondered, if his father asked him to perform a pass, would he be able to move? He felt his heart race with life. He swallowed, and swished his tongue in his dry mouth. "Am I to fight now, Papa?" he whispered.

Alvaro, Sr. didn't laugh. He spoke to his son softly, about fear.

"I'm not afraid to fight," Alvaro, Jr. answered.

"Shhh, shhh," his father hissed in reply. "*Chico estupido*, bulls are tested for their bravery, but they fight

14

only once. You know this. Bulls are smart, and they have memories. Would you ruin this fine animal before he has a chance to grow? No, this bull will grow to be a worthy opponent, as you will, too, Alvaro. Someday, perhaps, you will face each other, but only once will this fine animal perform the dance of death."

The party remained silent until Alvaro, Jr. and his father backed out of the small pen. They did not breathe their sighs of relief, or laugh at Alvaro, until the gate was again locked on the animal.

That afternoon, the men sat in the shade of a boojum tree, drinking wine, shelling nuts, negotiating the purchase of the bulls Alvaro, Sr. and his manager had decided to buy to face the matador in the ring in the coming season. The women sat in the cool of the long porch of the ranch's hacienda, around a large teak table, sipping Coca-Cola, talking softy, sewing. The children were supposed to be napping on mats on the floor of the ranch's main room, two ceiling fans humming above them, but Alvaro was too angry to sleep. He had stood, face-to-face, with his first bull that afternoon. Surely now he should be allowed to sit with the men while they spoke of the fine points of each of the animals and dickered over their price.

He closed his eyes when he saw his father come in the door of the hacienda, his mother following with his costume in her arms. He opened them again when he heard them emerge from a small room to the side of the main one where the children slept, his father resplendent in his tight new black satin trousers, his gold-embroidered cape. He rose from his mat to watch through the window as the seamstress fitted a black satin jacket with gold cording on his father's trim body.

That evening there was a party outdoors, neighbors coming to celebrate the famous matador and his family, and the magnificent sale that had been made to his manager, strands of red and green and gold lights twinkling over tables set up under the boojum tree, the savory scent of a pig roasting over a fire, a mariachi band playing while couples danced and drank, joss sticks for the children to wave as they played.

The more the grown-ups drank, the less attention they paid to the children. Alvaro, Jr. was able to wander away from the party. He jammed his joss stick into the dirt and headed for the corrals. His calf was still in its solitary pen and he stared into is glistening eyes from behind the safety of the field fence. "*Cabron*," he spat at the young bull as he picked a rock from the path and tossed it, hard, at the animal, who snorted as the rock connected with his chest. "*Cabron!*" Alvaro, Jr. spat again as the animal charged into the wire and the boy ran away.

The next morning, the men were again up early, drinking coffee and signing sales slips at the teak table on the hacienda porch. The women milled around the kitchen, tending children and preparing breakfast and one of them, the seamstress, was ironing Alvaro, Sr.'s new costume and packing it in a long, cloth bag for travel. "No, no, no," Alvaro, Jr. heard the seamstress say, and he turned his head to catch her prying Jorge's hands from the gold-corded jacket. "You will wrinkle it, *mocoso*!"

Alvaro, Jr. smiled. "I'll take him," he said.

The seamstress frowned.

"What a big boy," Mrs. Moreno said to her son. To the seamstress, she added, "He is old enough to take care of the little one."

"I'll take him for a walk," Alvaro, Jr. said.

"Be back in time for breakfast," his mother told him. "Half an hour, no more."

"I'll be back," Alvaro, Jr. assured her, and he walked quickly out of the magnificent kitchen, pushing the toddler before him. The men on the porch didn't even look up as the two children passed by.

Alvaro, Jr. walked the boy down the path and, where it forked, steered the boy in the direction of the barn. It would take them almost fifteen minutes to get to the corrals – Jorge's legs were so short, and he would not walk in a straight line, crisscrossing the path to pick a wildflower here, an interesting rock there. "Hurry up," Alvaro urged him. "We don't have much time and you want to see the bulls, don't you?"

Jorge smiled and nodded furiously.

"Then move it, *pequeño monstruo*!"

At the corrals, Alvaro, Jr. led Jorge to the little enclosure that held his calf. It was chilly in the morning air, and he watched the steam curl from the calf's nostrils while he waited for a lone ranch hand to decide a water trough was filled, turn off the pump and head back into the barn. Then he said to Jorge, "He's pretty, isn't he?" He waved a hand at the sleek animal.

Jorge grinned and nodded.

"And he's really soft. His fur is all silky. Have you ever petted a bull?"

Jorge grinned even wider, and shook his head.

"Would you like to pet one?"

Jorge giggled, nodding and jumping up and down.

"Well, go on, then. Under there," Alvaro said, kicking his foot toward the gap at the base of the field fence.

Jorge frowned. "Mama said no, not to go under there."

"Well, Mama's not here now, is she?" Alvaro said. "You saw me go in there yesterday. Don't you want to be a big boy like me and pet the bull?"

"Yes!" Jorge shrieked and, giggling, threw himself into the dust and rolled toward the gap.

Alvaro, Jr. smiled and bent to pick up a couple of rocks from the path. When Jorge was well into the pen, on his back, looking up at the calf with wild, wonder-filled eyes, Alvaro, Jr. took aim.

The children sat at the long table in the magnificent kitchen, silent, understanding even to the youngest one that they weren't welcome to make their presence known.

The women were gathered in the main room, the two ceiling fans humming softly overhead, the hum and the women's sobs drowned out by the wails and screams of the seamstress. Her husband, too shocked for tears, held her upright, tightly, as if this task was all that was keeping him on his feet too. The ranch hand who'd scooped up the boy and run with him to the hacienda still stood by the side of the leather sofa where he'd placed the body. The hand had been tossed when the calf had reared his head into his ribs. He thought at least one of the ribs was broken, and blood traced his features from the wound he'd sustained over his left eye when he'd landed.

The men sat at the teak table on the porch. "How did the boy get into the pen?" they asked Alvaro, Jr.. And, "Didn't you see him trying to crawl under the fence?" And, "You couldn't stop him?" And, "You shouldn't have tried to save him all by yourself!"

Alvaro, Sr. held a towel filled with ice to the side of his son's head, the gash over his right ear he'd taken when he tried to swing open the cattle gate and the calf had charged. "I had to try to save him," Alvaro, Jr. said. He looked up at his father. "I wasn't afraid to do it, Papa."

Alvaro, Sr. closed his eyes. The season before him was in jeopardy. His manager's son was dead. He was going to be no good for business for months ahead. And the wife, how could she be expected to finish fitting his new costumes now? He kept his eyes closed – he didn't want to look upon the world – but he said, "I know, Alvaro. You are a brave boy."

Alvaro, who was now, at last, among the men, turned his head toward his father's hand, the one that held the packet of ice to his ear, and buried his face in his father's arm. So the men wouldn't see him smile.

THE DEVIL'S FLEAS

Chicxulub, 1958

His mother was not a whore. Pablo Navarro was very specific on this point and he would have fought any of the other local boys to a bloody pulp if they would have had the nerve to say so.

She *could* have been a whore, Pablo allowed – she was beautiful enough to entice any man; Pablo often watched from a crack in her bedroom door as she sat at her dressing table preparing for the evening's business, a length of white cotton protecting her flowered chiffon gown as she applied her make-up – a ruby-red rouge she used both on her high cheekbones and on her voluptuous lips; an ink black pencil with which she outlined her eyes. As she pinned the flower Matilde brought in from the garden into her hair, a flower that always, *always*, matched the ones that cascaded on the fabric of her gown – bougainvillea, allamanda, wild lilies. As she dabbed the Guerlain L'heure Bleue perfume generously on the nape of her neck, and the insides of her elbows, and behind her knees.

"Pablo!" his mother would exclaim, laughing, when she caught him peeking through her door – and she always, *always*, caught him because the floors in the Navarro house always squeaked. Nobody ever noticed the squeaks when the house was filled with people, chatter and music. In these quiet moments, though, the loose floorboards were like little bombs that would detonate with each footfall. "Pablo! You go to check on the ice, please! Do your job."

There was never enough ice. The town of Chicxulub had been electrified for nearly twelve years, and his mother had lately installed a brand new, pale aqua blue Frigidaire refrigerator with Frost-Proof Freezing in the house's kitchen, but they went through a lot of ice. The gentlemen liked their whiskey on the rocks. Pablo's job was to empty, and then refill, the two dozen ice trays in the freezer at least three times a day, stocking the white enamel bowl on the freezer's top shelf with lots of rocks.

"What a good boy!" Matilde pinned Pablo's face between her two hands and covered his cheeks with kisses. Matilde was old – she had been his *grandmother's* maid; making ice in an electric box was still a novelty for her, and her old hands had trouble grasping the levers on the ice trays, and pulling them hard enough to release the cubes. She was genuinely grateful for his help, however his mother required it, and he allowed her this enthusiasm, squinting but not squirming beneath her barrage of kisses.

Pablo's mother routinely descended the central staircase in the house precisely an hour before the men began to arrive. She checked the rooms for dust and the beds for fresh linens. She inspected the girls for cleanliness – smelling their breath and their hands and their bosoms. She held up the crystal tumblers on the shelf in the bar to make sure they'd been polished, and she sampled the finger foods Matilde had laid out for their guests to snack upon, and then, at last, she would dim the lights, and spray the bulbs with a spritz of her Guerlain L'heure Bleue, and allow Pablo to fill the silver ice bucket with a supply from the white enamel bowl in the freezer. Then she would open her doors to the gentlemen.

The gentlemen who came to his mother's house were the most important men in Chicxulub – doctors and land owners, lawyers and planters, several famous matadors and one famous opera singer, councilmen and the municipal president himself, Rudolfo Hermida, who smoked fat cigars and dressed every day, head-to-toe, in crisp, sparkling white linen. They were very fond of *Señora* Navarro, calling her *bomboncita* and *mi corazón*. They brought her bottles of deep red wine for her table and bolts of flowered fabric for her gowns. Rudolfo Hermida himself brought her, over the years, many exotic rose bushes for her garden, which her neighbor, *Señora* Dzul, appreciated very much – *Señora* Dzul kept bees, her honey one of the Yucatan's most famous. Once, *Señor* Hermida had brought his mother an emerald ring she wore on the middle finger of her right hand. "The better to tell you what I think of you when you misbehave," *Señora* Navarro had said to him upon receiving it, extending the finger. Even Ned Achenbach, the poor American writer who'd come to live among them and find inspiration and couldn't afford to pay for her girls, brought her flowers from his window box and pieces of his poetry when he passed by her house on his afternoon walks. He couldn't speak much Spanish, but he brought Pablo and *Señora* Navarro's girls American candies, Junior Mints and Smarties and Mounds bars, and Pablo liked to talk with him and practice the English the nuns were trying to teach him in school. Even in his poverty, Ned was endeared to the mistress of the house. The other little boys in Pablo's elementary school knew that Pablo likely wasn't the only one who would beat them to a bloody pulp if they spoke disparagingly of his mother.

Once a week, at least – often more frequently – Pablo's fastidious mother conducted more random, and more thorough, examinations of her business and its assets. If she noticed a streak on a window, Matilde was instructed to call in a crew to wash all the windows, inside and out. If she noticed a spot of tarnish on the silver ice bucket, Matilde and Pablo and the girls were enlisted to polish every piece of silver in the house. When she spotted

Frieda, her newest girl, surreptitiously rubbing her *coño* under the table one afternoon over their early supper, Pablo's mother threw up the tablecloth, and the skirt of Freida's dress, and demanded Frieda show her *bizcocho*. Frieda was indignant, but *Señora* Navarro was insistent, and Matilde took one look at the *bizcocho* in question and declared, "The devil's fleas."

Matilde's joke made Pablo's mother laugh – the literal translation of the word Chicxulub was flea devil – so she batted Frieda about the head only three times, drawing only a little blood from her lower lip and otherwise causing no harm. Then she extended a hand to Frieda, to help her from the floor where she'd fallen when *Señora* Navarro had struck her, and the girls got to work. All the beds had to be stripped, the linens washed in boiling water. The upholstered furniture and deep pile rugs all through the house needed to be vacuumed and beaten. The girls all had to bathe with a special soap, and comb their *vello púbico* with a special comb.

And the gentlemen had to be told, which was the true nightmare.

"Who has hired her?" Matilde asked.

Pablo's mother gave a heavy sigh. "She is pretty, and young, and new. So many wanted to try her – and, oh, they will be so angry with us. How many of them have been with their wives since they have tried?"

It was a question that made Matilde gasp, and then immediately attempt to comfort both of them with the possibility that it could have been worse. *Sifilis*. *El embarazo*. Matilde crossed herself. "We are blessed it is only the itch. Only the itchy fleas."

"Mama?" Pablo was only twelve at the time, more sophisticated than most boys his age about the sort of topics under discussion yet still easily confused by them. He asked, "Mama, why do we need to tell the gentlemen at all, if they will be angry with us?"

Pablo's mother snorted. "Because if they do not clean their own fleas they will simply bring them back into my house the next time they visit. No, no, Pablo, if your house is dirty, you must clean it. Clean it all. You don't sweep dust under a rug, you take it outside and put it in the bin to be taken away."

Matilde nodded as Pablo's mother spoke, to endorse the view that she was speaking the truth. "We will need to know where Frieda got the fleas in the first place," she added.

"Oh, we will know," Pablo's mother said.

It had been unnecessary, Pablo thought, to make Frieda cry, his mother slapping her with a bamboo back scratcher she'd picked up once on a trip to America and making angry, red welts rise on the backs of Frieda's small, pale hands. "Not from our gentlemen," his mother spat, and *smack*! "Our gentlemen are upstanding citizens!" *Smack*! "Where did you pick up these fleas, *puta sucia*, and bring them into my house because you didn't get them from our good gentlemen!" *Smack, smack, smack*!

Pablo watched from a crack in the parlor door as his mother revealed the answer to this question to Rudolfo Hermida. His mother sat stiffly upright on a hard, dining room chair, and *Señor* Hermida sat in the wing-back chair by the window, the one with the maroon brocade and gold-painted lion's feet. He sat completely at his ease, the late afternoon sun brilliant as it flooded through the window behind him, resplendent in his trademark white linen suit, sipping from a heavy tumbler of his favorite whiskey *Señora* Navarro had poured for him over ice cubes Pablo had chipped special from their trays.

"I don't mind," Pablo's mother told *Senor* Hermida, "if she has a boyfriend, even some *sucio americano*, she can fuck for free all she wants on her own time. What she may not do is bring filth into my house."

Señor Hermida nodded at the wisdom of her words.

"And cause my gentlemen distress," Pablo's mother added and, at this, *Señor* Hermida snorted.

"There are wives all over Chicxulub today cursing their husbands as they clean *fleas*." He spat the last word, and shook his head, and Pablo saw his mother lower hers in response. He saw her humiliation. Her abject surrender. "What is the girl's punishment?" *Señor* Hermida asked.

Pablo's mother lifted her head. "I will take all her earnings, until all my costs for cleaning are met," she replied.

At this, *Señor* Hermida snorted again. "You think she will have much earnings? Who do you think will have her now?"

Pablo's mother blinked several times, against the sun shining behind *Señor* Hermida. "I myself have assured that she is clean."

Señor Hermida replied with an operatic shrug.

Pablo's mother cleared her throat. "And the boy? The American? What will you do to him, Rudolfo?"

Señor Hermida took another long drink of his whiskey. "What do you think I should do with him, *bomboncita*?"

"I think you should kill him," Pablo's mother snapped, which sent *Señor* Hermida laughing so hard he rocked back in the wing-back chair. "And why not?" she demanded. "He is killing my business! He has ruined my best girl! An eye for an eye!"

Señor Hermida continued to chuckle even while he soothed her. "Now, there, *mi corazón*, remember: the punishment should be in proportion to the crime!"

Pablo's mother grew abruptly still. *Señor* Hermida's laughter petered out into a silence only he was comfortable with. Pablo would have liked to back away from the door, pretend he hadn't seen any of it, but he was afraid the floor would squeak.

"Pablo!" He heard the legs of his mother's hard chair scrape on the floorboards as she turned toward the door to call to him. "Go get more ice. *Señor* Hermida would like more ice for his drink. Get more ice, and tell Matilde to bring some little sandwiches. *Señor* Hermida and I will have a few little sandwiches while we talk!" Pablo heard the chair scrape again as his mother returned her attention to her guest. "*Señor* Hermida and I have much to talk about, and settle between us – "

The late afternoons in Merida were lazy. Pablo would return home from school and sit at the table in the kitchen eating the little sandwiches Matilde had prepared for him, drinking a glass of cola, doing his homework. He was a smart boy and homework was never a long endeavor. There were typically at least two hours to kill before his mother began dressing for the evening, and the girls came down for their early supper, and he was needed to take care of the ice.

This afternoon everything was off schedule, what with *Señor* Hermida's visit. His mother had put on her gown in the middle of the afternoon, and called for ice well before the evening Angelus. Pablo finished a particularly challenging word problem in his math book, closed his schoolbooks and set them aside.

"You are still hungry?" Matilde asked him, clearing his sandwich plate and his empty glass.

"No, Matilde. Thank you." Pablo tipped his chair back on two legs while he thought. "I think I'm going to go for a walk, Matilde."

"Go, go," Matilde told him. "Be back in time for ice. We will need more ice before the gentlemen arrive."

"Back in plenty of time for ice."

The American, Ned Achenbach, lived in two, ground-floor rooms off an alleyway two blocks from *Señora* Navarro's house. The rooms were small, but Ned kept them tidy and the window in the main room was rather large so the room got a surprising amount of sun. When Pablo arrived, Ned was sitting on the one stair that led to the entry of his hovel.

"Wow," Pablo said.

"Aw, it's not so bad," Ned said. He switched the bag of ice he was holding over his eye from his right hand to his left, so he could fish the Mounds bar out of his shirt pocket and hand it to Pablo.

"Thanks," Pablo said.

Ned shrugged. "I was going to run it by before your mother opened for business tonight, but I think I wouldn't be welcome."

"Probably not," said Pablo, removing the wrapper from the candy. Mounds were his favorite.

"Hey, so, do you know why Hermida's goons jumped me?"

Pablo nodded and swallowed a mouthful of Mounds before he spoke. "Frieda."

Ned raised the eyebrow over his good eye.

"Because you gave her fleas."

"*Fleas?*"

"You know – " Pablo used a forefinger to make a circular motion around his crotch.

Ned cocked his head. "I have no idea what you're talking about." He removed the ice bag from his eye and Pablo whistled.

"The goons. They got you good."

Ned tried to open the injured eye, but winced as it proved too painful. "I still don't know if I can see out of it or not." He put the ice bag back on his face. "Maybe when Frieda gets up you can translate for us, she was just rambling and crying when she got here – "

"Frieda's here?"

"She showed up half an hour ago, right after the goons left, hysterical. All I could figure out was your mother fired her and she's sorry about something. I gave her a shot of whiskey to calm her down. She's in my bed sleeping it off."

Pablo nodded, it made sense to him that Frieda was in Ned's bed, but then he frowned. "Are you and Frieda going to get married now?" he asked.

He was startled by how hard Ned began to laugh.

"What? Isn't that what people do? You know, when they get to be your age?"

Ned was still laughing so hard he could barely hold the ice bag to his face. Pablo had to look away from the raw meat that was his left eye.

"You think Frieda and I – " He gasped, howled, caught his breath. "Frieda and me?"

Pablo's frown deepened so much it almost began to hurt. "That's what she told my mother…"

"Huh," Ned grunted, still chuckling. "Whadda ya know? I'm Frieda's beard too," he muttered, and hooted.

Pablo chewed another bite of Mounds.

Ned put the bag of ice back on his eye.

A few of *Señora* Dzul's honey bees buzzed around the flower boxes in front of Ned's large window on their way back to her hive.

"Frieda doesn't have a beard," Pablo said, and made Ned start laughing all over again.

WAR

The two rich boys – Jack Cohen, the banker's son, and the other one, Clint Kennedy, who might as well have been the banker's son, the way the Cohen family treated him – had little use for the Cruet children who had invaded the Cohens' large, cool kitchen. Charlotte heard Candace Cohen, the skinny, sweet smelling woman who was her father's employer, whisper to the two boys, "Just look after them for the morning." The other woman, Mrs. Kennedy, who was also Mrs. Cohen's employee, Charlotte had been told, but who looked and carried herself as if she was Mrs. Cohen's friend, added, shaking her head, "Their mother is in the hospital again."

It wasn't out of the ordinary that the two boys would have no use for the little children – even at just nine years old, Charlotte understood this; the boys were fourteen, soon to be fifteen. They'd been expecting to spend this summer morning playing video games and splashing in the Cohens' pool and riding their bikes through Homestead to the dairy for their handmade ice cream sandwiches, not babysitting the gardener's kids.

There were four kids, total – Charlotte and her three younger brothers: Chester, Jr., five, known as Junie; Tomas, four, called Tom-Tom; and baby Kenneth, Kenny, not quite three but already almost as tall as Tom-Tom. The teenagers' video games were too violent for the younger ones, the pool too dangerous, and, well, no one had even suggested the two boys haul their little charges into town for ice cream.

"What would you like to do?" Jack knelt down and gamely asked the Cruet children.

Charlotte knew her bothers would be too shy too reply, so she thought through the answer for them. She generally liked to play house with her brothers – she pretended they were her children and she their mother, and she was such a jolly mommy the boys never failed to go along with her game. Now, though, with her mother in the hospital again –

She had heard the talk, whispers between her father and Mrs. Cohen – *breast cancer, metastasis, can the chemo work a second time?* Playing house now made her feel queasy, as if it wasn't play but a rehearsal for a part she'd eventually be called on to fulfill in real life. The idea of having a house, even a make-believe one, felt suffocating to her – she'd heard *those* whispers too, between her parents, in their native Spanish: her mother's nearly desperate plea, *"How will we be able to keep the house if I'm not working? Where will the money come from?"* And her father's reply – automatic, and not entirely convincing, *"You don't worry about that. I will bring in the money we need. You are to think only of getting well."*

Charlotte had come to think of a house as a fragile thing, easily lost, with something to fear lurking at each turn. Lately even her favorite part of the day – gathered with her family around the kitchen table after dinner so she could teach them all the finer points of the English language she alone seemed able to master – had lost its joy.

Besides, if they played house, what roles would she assign to the two big boys? The handsome one, Clint Kennedy, could be her husband easily enough, but what would she do with Jack Cohen?

We could go out into the yard to play, she thought. The redwood playset with swings and a slide and a sandbox that had long ago been installed for the big boys still stood, neglected now, mostly, except for the rare days on which her father brought her or one of her brothers with him while he worked in the Cohens' gardens. Charlotte paused – had her father ever before brought all four of them to the Cohen house on the same day? She thought not, which only proved to her how serious and extraordinary her mother's hospitalization was this time.

"Charlotte?" Jack Cohen said to her, pulling her back from the sadness threatening her. "What are you thinking?"

"That it's too hot to go outside to play," she replied. Tom-Tom hung from one of her hands, Kenny from the other, and even Junie who, at five, thought himself more independent of her than the other two, slipped behind her and rested his forehead against her back.

"It is," Jack agreed. "Way too hot. So, what else would you like to do?"

Honestly, Charlotte thought, *I could entertain myself all morning just walking around and looking into the rooms in this house.*

The little two-bedroom bungalow Charlotte and her brothers shared with their parents could fit into the Cohens' kitchen. She thought that being allowed to explore would be like wandering through a castle, discovering new treasures at every turn, one bright, glorious room after the next. The very idea made her heart swell with envy and ambition, though such activity would bore her brothers, and never be sanctioned even if she could summon the nerve to ask. She wondered, though, if, as Mrs. Kennedy and her son had been invited to do when Mr. Kennedy had gone, she and her brothers and her father would be invited to move into the Cohen house when her mother was gone, too. The thought was fantastic – she wanted most of all to live in a house like this, but not without her mother. And yet, why did these people need all of these rooms? Surely there were more than enough rooms in this castle, even if her mother came along with them. This knowledge brought her close to tears of sorrow. And rage.

"We could watch television in the TV room," Jack offered, gesturing somewhere off the kitchen. "Cartoons? Do you like cartoons? Or, if not, I'm sure my mother has a stash of crayons and drawing paper somewhere, maybe up in the sewing room. I could go look if you think you'd like to draw? Or, you know…" – his brow furrowed as he fought to come up with a third option – "maybe, do you like foosball? There's a table down in the rec room – "

"Or," Clint jumped in while Jack was still eyeing the children, concluding that the oldest girl was the only one among them who was even tall enough to properly reach the foosball table, "maybe we can all get up a good game of poker? Didn't your dad have his friends over last night, Jackie? I'll bet the card table is still set up in the blue living room and that this little girl could take us for everything we have on us."

The big boys laughed at this notion.

"How much do you have on you?" Charlotte asked them.

The blue living room – the living room that was to the right of the grand staircase, just off the foyer – was, in Charlotte's estimation, a room for a real princess. There was a fireplace of white-painted brick at the far end, with a huge painting of the smiling Cohen family hanging above. It was flanked by two, long, soft white sofas and, between them, a glass table set on a base of gilded wrought iron leaves. There was a huge, white, baby grand piano at the other end of the room, and a tall, glass-fronted case filled with photographs of Jack Cohen and his older brother Abe, and Clint Kennedy too, in fancy frames, and a fat, gray leather rhinoceros set before one of two wingback chairs upholstered in pale blue silk. Huge, crystal vases filled with flowers cut from her father's gardens sat on almost every table. A folding card table was still set up before one of the sets of French doors that led to a wide, brick patio, and the rose garden beyond, and still covered with the white cloth Mrs. Kennedy had draped over it for Mr. Cohen's poker party the night before. The cloth was a bit rumpled, though the men's ashtrays and snack plates and tumblers had been removed from it, but it was still remarkably clean in spite of all that. A carousel of poker chips still sat on top, along with a deck of cards, a couple of pencils, and one of Mrs. Cohen's monogrammed notepads for keeping score. The whole room was painted a color Charlotte had once heard Mrs. Cohen say was "robin's egg blue" and it still smelled faintly of the men's cigars.

"You sure you know how to play?" Jack laughed as Charlotte took a seat in one of the four chairs around the card table.

"You go sit on that couch," Charlotte told her brothers. "Sit still and be quiet," she instructed them and, to the astonishment of Jack and Clint, the little boys quietly obeyed. "Good boys," she told them. The ceilings were so high overhead her voice echoed. She turned to the big boys. "I know how to play War," she answered Jack.

The rules for the game of War are very simple – so simple a child can play. A pack of cards is divided in half and one half is set, face down, before each of two players. At the same time, the players turn over the top card on their individual piles and the person who has the higher card takes them both. If the cards match – two threes or two queens, for example – then "war" is declared and each player deals three cards, face down, and one card, face up, and whoever has the higher card takes them all. The game ends when one player ends up with all the cards. Aces are high.

Neither Clint nor Jack had played War in years – not since they were much younger children – but, given that neither of them were any more sure of the rules of poker than Charlotte, Jack sat down at the card table across from Charlotte and cheerfully cut the cards, taking one of the resulting halves for himself and sliding the other pile over the rumpled white cloth toward the little girl. "What should we play for?" he asked.

"A dollar for every time we win war," Charlotte replied, as if she'd already thought all this out. "And a five for whoever wins at the end of the whole thing."

Jack chuckled. "High stakes. Do you have any money?"

The question made Charlotte blush a furious red.

"Then what will you give me when you lose?" Both big boys laughed at the question.

Charlotte glared at them. "I won't lose," she told them, which only made the boys laugh harder.

"Your funeral," Jack said and then, remembering the sorrowful reason the little children were at his house in

the first place, he hurriedly added, "Let's go. Let's play."
He turned up the first card in his pile.

In the first hand, Jack turned up a five and Charlotte
a six; in the second, Jack turned up a ten, and Charlotte
a jack; in the third Jack turned up a four and Charlotte
an ace. And then they both turned up kings and war was
declared, Charlotte winning with a four against Jack's
two. The teenager groaned but fished a dollar out of his
back pocket and handed it over to the little girl.

A mere ten minutes and twelve dollars later, Charlotte
sat at the card table, the little boys jumping and cheering
around her chair, all of them beaming as she counted her
winnings. Jack sat on the arm of one of the white sofas,
where Clint had slumped for the duration of the game.
"Did she cheat?" he whispered.

Clint shrugged. "And after her fifth war victory in a
row I started to pay attention."

"I didn't win *once*," Jack complained. "Doesn't that
seem fishy to you?

Clint nodded. "Of course it does."

Jack watched as Charlotte stuffed the wad of his five
and ones under the tongue of her tightly laced sneaker.
"Should we say something?"

Clint shrugged again. "It's just a few dollars. Maybe
she's just lucky."

Jack snorted and sank down onto the sofa next to
Clint. "Someday her luck will run out," he predicted.

"Knock it off." Clint backhanded him in the stomach and laughed as Jack groaned – *Ooof* – and doubled over. "Her mom's sick – she doesn't have much of any other kind of luck working for her right now. What's a few dollars here and there to you?"

After War, Mrs. Kennedy found them all in the blue living room. She set them all up at the table in the breakfast nook with drawing paper and crayons, the teenagers supervising. When Kenny grew cranky and tired of coloring, she turned on the hose on the kitchen patio and made up a game of limbo, the spray of water substituting for the stick, and left the big boys to referee. When the little ones were soaked through, she brought out towels and rubbed Charlotte dry while Jack and Clint toweled off the little boys and ushered them all back into the kitchen for lunch – BLTs, and bowls of cut-up bananas, and orange sodas.

"Can we go?" Clint asked his mother when they were done eating. "Can we be off duty now?" He rolled his eyes at the kids.

"Go on then," Mrs. Kennedy said, waving the teenagers off with a manicured hand, the nails the same blood-red color as Mrs. Cohen's.

Clint snickered – not at her, but at Jack – when he saw the nail polish. Mrs. Cohen often treated his mother to a manicure on the days her aesthetician came to the house to change her color. "Is that why we had to watch the Cruet kids today? So you could get your nails done?" he asked, incredulous.

By the end of the day his mother would have removed her color, complaining that it wouldn't last anyway. That manicures were an inconvenience for a woman with work to do.

"I said, go on then," Mrs. Kennedy snapped back at him, and the big boys rushed out of the kitchen before she could change her mind. They made a quick pitstop in Mrs. Cohen's sewing room, where her dressmaker was fitting a gown she wanted to wear that weekend to a Red Cross fundraiser, so Jack could ask for money to replace what he'd lost at cards. Mrs. Cohen was pinned into her new garment and had no patience to hear their tale of how Jack's money had been lost in the first place, so she asked them only to hand her purse to her and then gave them all she had on hand – a fifty-dollar bill.

Jack and Clint had already spent the hours of their afternoon with friends in Homestead, at the dairy treating everyone to ice cream and games in the arcade across the street, when Mr. Cruet washed the last dirt of the day from his hands at the sink in the gardening shed and came to the house to collect his children. The boys weren't around to hear him thank Mrs. Cohen and Mrs. Kennedy for taking care of his family while he worked, nor to hear the women reply, "No, thank *you* for lending us these lovely children for the day!"

They weren't there to see Charlotte help her father load her brothers into the back seat of their old, wood-paneled station wagon, and strap Kenny into his car seat, and take up her mother's place in the front seat for herself. Or to see her pull Jack's wad of cash from under the tongue of her sneaker and hand it to her father and say, "For the house, *Papi*. So we can keep the house." Or to hear him ask her, "Where did you come by this money?"

They weren't there to hear her answer, or witness Chester Cruet spit out the door of his car to demonstrate how he felt about gamblers and their ill-gotten gains. Or to see him leave his little boys in the back of the station wagon and march his daughter back into Cohen house and make her hand over her winnings to Mrs. Cohen. They weren't there that afternoon to witness Charlotte's tears of humiliation as she apologized to Jack's and Clint's mothers for taking their sons' allowances in a game of cards.

And they weren't there four years later – they were in college by that time – to witness her tears of sorrow when Mrs. Cruet finally lost her battle with cancer.

They weren't there fifteen years later, either – Jack was working for his father's bank by then, and Clint was already in Mexico, making his own fortune – when Charlotte came by the Cohen house to pick up her father in the old, wood-paneled station wagon at the end of his workday. Mr. Cohen happened to be in the garden talking to Mr. Cruet about a crack he'd found in the pool that needed to be repaired when Charlotte pulled into the driveway and tooted for her father. Mr. Cohen marveled at what a beauty Charlotte had become – "I haven't seen you in, what, dear? Ten years?" he'd said to her, And he smiled at Mr. Cruet's beaming face when the gardener told him his daughter was now in college, studying to be a teacher, and, on a whim, Mr. Cohen asked Charlotte if she needed a job to help her through school.

"My children are always looking for good work," Mr. Cruet replied for her and Mr. Cohen hired her on the spot as a part-time secretary for his eldest son, Abe, who was also now working at the bank and needed help, Mr. Cohen believed, to stay organized.

Jack and Clint weren't there on her first day of work at the bank, when Abe plugged her into the bank's computer system so she could input information on the loan applications he'd handed off to her. They didn't see her stifle a laugh when she realized how brazenly Abe was doctoring his clients' financials. They didn't see her eyes well up with happy tears, didn't know that her heart swelled with envy and ambition as she realized how easy it would be to divert a few dollars here and there to an account of her own. Not a lot. Maybe just enough to pass off to her father as her own earnings, so he could finally pay off the mortgage on their little bungalow.

Maybe just a little more to pay off her student loans.

Just a few dollars, here and there.

SAFE

Northampton, Massachusetts, 1967

A little background: most people had no idea that Candace Cohen's maiden name was originally Leland. She'd been only five months old, after all, when Harold James Leland was arrested and arraigned, and just shy of a year and half when his trial had ended and he'd been thrown in jail for forty-four years. Her mother, Adele, who had been sullied right along with her husband – but only because she had been married to him – had been adamant that her only child would not bear the undue burden of carrying the bastard's name.

For a brief period – seven months – Adele had reverted to using her own maiden name for herself and her daughter, but soon enough she had remarried. While a Leland, Adele had been a glittering fixture of Atlanta society, but she had moved back to her far less glamourous hometown of Charlotte, North Carolina after the divorce and done whatever had been required of her to fit back into the local scene. That included marrying the son of a small-town bigshot, the banker and golf club champion, Stuart Kunstler. The boy, named Horace, who was commonly, and kindly, known as Buck. Yes, Buck's parents were a bit hard to take. Buck's father was too proud of his golf club trophies, and his mother too protective of the son she'd too recently welcomed back from war, and she was not over the moon about the fact that her first grandbaby was going to be another man's child. And, yes, Buck's sketchy teenage brother, Walt, was a bit of a wild card from whom one might expect some sort of scandal or another as he grew into a man. But Buck himself had adored Adele Joy Zucker ever since he'd spotted the cheeky blonde high-school freshman on the first day of his senior year.

Adele couldn't have been more pleased that her second husband was going to be in all ways so very opposite of her first. The Klieg lights of high society had burned her once; the hazy glow of local celebrity had become more than enough to satisfy her.

In short order, both Adele and Candace became well settled into Buck's identity, fully Kunstlers. Even Adele's suspicious mother-in-law was won over, if not by Adele then by her charming child. Over the years, most other people in the small town easily forgot that Candace wasn't her stepfather's biological child. This was not hard to do when they saw Buck walking hand-in-hand with little Candy down the town's main street, on their way to the florist to buy roses for Adele's birthday, or to the candy shop to buy chocolates for his wife on Valentine's Day. They would smile as father indulged daughter in a few candies for herself at the candy store counter. Very few townsfolk even made the effort to whisper, passing the gossip on to the next generation, when Candace's brothers began arriving, one after the other, regular as clockwork, every two years for the following six years.

"What a handsome family," people would say when they saw them all together at the country club and at temple. "Four kids," an old man at temple laughed, "a real mensch, and busy!"

"Don't this little girl look just like her daddy," the new waitress at the club gushed. And in a happy twist of fate, the little girl did look remarkably like Buck Kunstler. She had his pale skin and his high cheekbones. And his long fingers. Candace never asked about any other father – she assumed Buck – and Adele breathed a sigh of relief; she had married well at last, and that first, disgusting martial mistake was going to be in jail for the rest of his life. She and Candace had landed on their feet.

So, seventeen years and two months later, in the early fall of 1967, when Hal Leland was released from prison – for good behavior, or because he was considered rehabilitated, or because of prison overcrowding and they were letting out non-violent offenders, or because of whatever bullshit Buck's attorney was trying to pass off as reasonable – the force of Adele's rage nearly shattered glass.

"Please, Adele," Buck purred at her, folding her in his arms and holding her very tightly and making *shh-shh-shh* noises in her ear so she would quiet down. They were sitting in the staid, heavily wood-paneled offices of the Kunstler family attorney; Buck was both sympathetic to and embarrassed by his wife's outburst. "It was good of him to give us the courtesy of being informed," Buck said to the attorney.

"Well – " the attorney said. "That's not all. Not just courtesy."

"What, then?" Buck asked.

The attorney ran a finger under his shirt collar. "He wants to see Candace."

Both the attorney and Buck braced for another ear-piercing wail from Adele, but she surprised them. "Over my fucking dead body," she growled.

Which was why, the first time Candace met with Hal Leland, Adele knew nothing about it. Candace was up north, in college, doing her sophomore year at Smith. The college was too far from the family seat as far as Adele was concerned, but what were you going to do if the kid had her heart set on it, Buck had asked. And so, when the dorm phone rang, one of the other girls had picked it up and shouted, without real thought, for "*Candy!*" when the caller asked for her.

Hal Leland took a seat in a booth at the back of Henry's Lunch and nursed a black coffee while he waited for his daughter to arrive. Not that talking her into coming to meet him had been a walk in the park.

"Who are you again?" she'd said into the dorm room phone.

"Leland," Hal had repeated. "Harold Leland."

"And that's supposed to mean what to me?" Candace had asked. Even as a college sophomore, Candace was not a pushover.

And that cut Hal badly. "I'm your father, Candy," he replied.

"My what?" Candace laughed so loudly a few of the other girls who were studying in the common room lifted their heads and looked at her.

"Your *father*," Hal insisted, but Candace had continued to laugh and that had pissed him off. "What year were Adele and Buck married, little girl? What year were you born? What city were you born in, and why do you think you were born in Atlanta and not in that one-horse shithole you live in now like your little... *brothers*? Jesus Christ, how did you not figure this out yourself? How'd you end up at Smith, a stupid girl like you?"

Candace was still undaunted. "Well," she'd demanded, "if you're my father, where have you been all my life?"

"In jail, sweetheart. But I'm out now."

Candy had grabbed her coat against the early October chill and rushed to the library, the periodicals room, the Microfiche machine. She worked backwards in time so the first article she came upon, in the Charlotte Observer, was from the January 23rd, 1948 issue. "Harold James Leland Sentenced to Forty-four Years," the headline read.

Following a four-month trial during which Harold James "Hal" Leland, once a pillar of Atlanta society, steadfastly maintained his innocence, Leland was sentenced today in Fulton County, Georgia to forty-four years behind bars for financial crimes including fraud and embezzlement as well as, more notoriously, the crime of statutory rape...

Candace had gasped, her hands flew to cover her mouth. The red, Shetland wool cardigan she'd been wearing over her shoulders fell to the floor of the periodicals room. If the man who'd called her at the dorm was, indeed, Hal Leland – and why would he choose such an infamous pseudonym if he wasn't who he said he was? – then he was a danger to her. Paternity notwithstanding, a rapist had called to talk to her out of the blue –

Except, *was* he her father?

Leland's wife, the former Adele Joy Zucker, has relocated to Charlotte, North Carolina in the wake of the verdict with the couple's infant daughter.

Candace thought she might vomit.

"I am completely innocent of all charges," Hal had said to her when they were on the phone. "No matter what your mother tells you, no matter what you might read about me, I am completely innocent."

But Adele hadn't told her anything. On the subject of fathers, all Adele had ever said was "You're a lucky girl, Candy. You have the best father in the world." Meaning Buck Kunstler. And for nearly two decades, Candace had believed that was true.

"Seven AM tomorrow morning, at Henry's Lunch," Candace said to Hal when she'd called him back upon her return from the library. "I have an eight o'clock biology lab, so seven. Sharp."

"I'll look forward to it," Hal told her and rang off.

Hal had arrived at Henry's Lunch early. Now he watched a beautiful young woman with his high cheekbones and her mother's slender fingers walk tentatively into the restaurant, holding the door open behind her with one arm as if she were afraid to commit to entering. She was wearing a crisp white blouse and an orange mohair cardigan over a pair of brown-and-mustard-yellow plaid wool Bermuda shorts, and a pair of chocolate-brown penny loafers with white knee socks. An orange grosgrain ribbon held her blonde hair off her face. Hal caught her eye, and waved. Candace stood still for a moment, transfixed. Then she turned and ran out the door. Hal stood, so he could keep Candace in his sight even for a moment longer, but all he saw was a blur of orange mohair through Henry's greasy front window as she fled down the street.

It wasn't easy getting from Northampton, Massachu-setts to Charlotte, North Carolina – a cab and a plane, and another plane, and then another cab and hours and hours.

"Did he do it, Mom? That's all I'm asking."

Adele sat at the dining room table, the tumbler of whisky Buck had brought to her sitting almost exactly midway between the two, shining silver candelabra. "I wanted to tell you."

"That's not what I'm asking – "

Adele sipped her whiskey with a trembling hand, her fury about the bastard having the balls to contact her daughter contained only by real fear of her daughter's anger. "And what was the point of telling you? You have a wonderful father, you have a wonderful life. You never needed him!"

"Did he do it?"

"*We* never needed him!"

Candy slammed the dining room table so hard with her fist that the ice rattled in her mother's glass. "Did he do any of it!"

"I don't know! I think he did, he must have, the police thought he did, a jury believed he did, but what's the difference? What's the difference, Candy? Whatever he did or did not do... It ruined us!"

Buck Kunstler listened to his wife cry from behind the swinging door that led into their kitchen. He listened to the woman he had come to love sob into her whiskey.

He listened to the wrath of the daughter he adored. Her shrill words of rage and confusion. At the end of the day, he was useless to both of them if he couldn't protect them. No matter what he had provided to them over nearly twenty years, even if he had done all that had been in his power, he had failed to protect them from Leland.

Hal Leland sat on the edge of the bed in his motel room. It wasn't bad, as rooms go in roadside motels: clean, if threadbare. It had a bed, a chair, a lamp, a TV, now playing the news on NBC – Huntley and Brinkley, Ali KOs Folley, the USSR performs nuclear tests in Eastern Kazakh, U Thant releases a proposal for peace in Vietnam – though he wasn't watching.

He hadn't wanted anything from his daughter, Candace, who now called herself by another man's last name, nothing but to see her again and, he supposed, he'd accomplished that. He'd gotten a good look at her, wide-eyed and scared to death, before she'd turned and run out of Henry's Lunch as if he was some sort of creepy-looking freak. Which – he shrugged – maybe he was. "Freak" was a word one could probably substitute for "felon". Someone outside the norm. Someone normal, upstanding citizens should avoid. Though – and here he laughed – one would have to leave "creepy-looking" out of the assessment. Hal Leland was a handsome man, and he knew it, and, after all those years in jail with nearly nothing to do but exercise, he was lean and fit and, quite possibly, even better looking than when he'd first gone into lock-up. He laughed again: *Man, does my daughter look like me or what? Cheekbones that could cut ice.*

More than anything he wanted a drink – a shot of whiskey, or two – but he hadn't had one of those in nineteen years and two months. He'd never drunk to excess, but why break his record now? Frankly, he attributed being off the sauce to the very appealing hard edge his good looks had taken over the last two decades, and he wasn't going to blow his looks now that he was free. He'd already wasted too many years of them behind bars.

Still, his kid had been repulsed by him and a nice whiskey would really soothe that burn.

Hal fished a bottle of Coke out of a paper bag, and dug around under the other, still chill bottles to find the church key he'd also bought at a little, local grocery store. *No Coke in jail*, he thought as he chugged, *and that was something I truly missed.*

Coke, and my kid.

He didn't know why he'd been so mean to his kid when he got her on the phone. *Stupid*, he'd called her, that perfect baby he loved. Who had once loved him. He rested his elbows on his knees and bowed his head. Had he expected her to rush to him after all these years, thrilled to have him back in her life? No. No, he hadn't expected that, but she hadn't even known who he was. Her bitch of a mother had never even told her who he was!

Which – he raised his head and took another long swig of his Coke – wasn't his kid's fault. *I should never have taken my anger about that out on my kid*, he thought, and shook his head. He wasn't forgiving himself for the things he'd said to Candace, only supposing that it was more than his looks that had taken on a hard edge in prison.

He unfolded himself from the bed and loped toward the door. It was cold outside. Really cold. But the cold felt good. He leaned against the frame of the open door and looked out into the motel parking lot, the turquoise neon sign in the middle of it that blinked and buzzed.

"Are you insane?" Walter Kunstler wanted to know. Walt, Buck's younger brother, was the only reason he had consented to allowing Candace to go to a school as far away from home as Smith. Walt lived in Boston, in a hundred-and thirty-year-old, five-bedroom brownstone on Pinckney Street. He was well-equipped, and local enough, to look after Candy when she went up North, Buck had promised his wife.

"I don't like your brother," Adele had replied.

Buck had smiled, a small, sad thing. "I know you don't – "

"There's something about him I find... unsavory."

"I know, I know, but he's family. And he'd do anything for Candy. You have to know that." Buck had stroked his wife's hand, cajoling her. "He's like all the

Kunstler men, just a fool for a beautiful woman," he'd added, and made Adele grin.

"Completely sane," Buck assured his brother now. "Do you know someone or not?"

Walt had left Charlotte in 1951, the week after his high-school graduation. His older brother had already served admirably in the U. S. Army 97th Infantry Division, Pacific Theater, and come immediately home to complete his undergraduate degree, with honors and in only three years, at North Carolina State. Buck had returned from Raleigh, degree in hand, and hung it essentially the next day on the wall in his office at the bank, the one just two doors down from their father's corner suite, and been working ever since. He bought a brick house in a fine, if not *the* very finest part of Charlotte, and started to look for the right wife to fill it with kids. Adele Zucker had come along at just the perfect moment.

Walt had wanted nothing to do with any of that – not the army, not N.C. State, not any bank other than one that would loan him money. He moved to Boston, took the first job he could find – fixing arcade games for the largest distributor in the city – and would have lived happily ever after except that he ended up doing very well in the arcade game business. He'd bought the distribution rights to the games, expanded the business statewide, and then into Vermont and New York, and finally into Ottawa. He spent too much time on the road, taking care of business, to date any nice girls – only a pro in a hotel room every now and then – and, by the time he realized maybe he did want a life more like his big brother's than not, he'd already met that family out of Queens. The men who told him, in so many words, that it was his choice – launder their money for them of his own free will or end up being convinced to do it from a hospital bed.

Anyway, it was how he was able to afford the brownstone on Pinckney Street, and he was still healthy.

"Do I know someone?" he laughed when his brother asked.

Buck waited now, sipping a cup of black coffee, for his wife and daughter to get up for the day. Adele, he knew, had had a lot of whiskey the night before – he'd whistled when he checked the level in the bottle this morning – so she wouldn't be climbing out of bed until at least mid-morning, if even that early, but Candy was sleeping off only rage.

The way she'd told the story last night, she'd never even really met Hal Leland. She'd tried to meet him, but her nerve had failed her and she'd rushed home to him, to the place she felt most safe in the world. There was no way she'd want to try to contact Leland even if she did have a telephone number for wherever it was he was staying now that he was out of prison. However she felt about being deceived about Hal's very existence, she would, like Adele, come to see his silence as a blessing. Eventually she'd stop wondering why he never tried to call her again. If she would ever wonder about that at all.

Sela, the weekday maid at the Northampton Motor Lodge and Apartments, wheeled her carts down the narrow concrete balcony in front of the second-floor rooms. One cart was filled with clean linens and had an empty laundry bag tied to one end of it; the other cart was stocked with cleaning supplies – a broom and a vacuum cleaner, a lot of Windex and rags, a bottle of Comet for the toilets and a squirt container of dishwashing liquid for the drinking glasses, and some spot remover for the rugs, if she needed it. Sela rarely needed it. Windex worked just fine for the windows and the laminated furniture in the rooms, and even the damned drinking glasses. Squirt a little Windex down inside, and on any lip marks at the rim, wipe it all up with a rag and good as new. No need to bother with sudsy water in the bathroom sink no matter what the owner's wife said.

Sela liked to start on the second floor, at the far end, and work her way down and back toward the front office. She plucked the master key from the side pocket of her stiff, new turquoise uniform – "Which matches our sign!" the owner's wife had said with delight when she gave it to her – and passed Room #210 on her way down the concrete balcony to her first clean-up of the day. She sighed when she saw the door to Room #210 was standing open.

Not cracked, but fully open.

"Shit," Sela muttered.

She entered Room #210 and looked around. The TV was on. *The Today Show*. Hugh Downs. There was a crumpled paper bag on the bed – two warm Cokes, Sela found when she looked inside – and, on the night table beside it, a cap from a bottle and a church key. Someone had sat on the bed, and leaned against the pillows, but it had not been slept in. There was no suitcase in sight. No discarded clothing or used towels on the floor. No wallet or set of keys on top of the desk. Sela glanced toward the bathroom door, behind which she distinctly heard water running, and she saw the door was closed. She walked over to it and knocked.

"Hey, Mister, check out was at eleven o'clock. You're supposed to be gone by now, I gotta clean the room."

When there was no answer, she knocked again. "Hey! Mister!" And when, again, there was no answer, she jiggled the handle, and when the door didn't open she inserted her master key in the lock and muttered, "Shit, they don't pay me enough for this."

NOWHERE

There was nowhere in the wide world that was safe. This Pedro knew without a glimmer of doubt though he had never in his life been more than twenty or thirty miles from his home in Merida. This unavoidable proximity to random danger was why for all of his twenty-one years and two months on this Earth he had kept his hands busy and his head low.

He had loved his job working for Mr. Clint. For nearly two years he had worked keeping Mr. Clint's house – had started working there even before it was a real home, when it was just another run-down palace on the *Paseo de Montejo* and the gringo had first arrived and begun to make it look like new again. Mr. Clint had come to live in the old palace with a boy, Mr. Taavi, a Mayan, which Pedro had found confusing. Even the dirt poor, like Pedro's family, had been above these Mayan savages – this was simply a thing that was understood – but Mr. Clint had brought the boy into his home and introduced Pedro to him with the honorific, as he might introduce a businessman or a politician. As if he expected Pedro would use it whenever he spoke of him.

At first, while spitting *Mr. Taavi* out of his mouth had angered him – and Pedro had never told his family this humiliation was required of him – Mr. Clint had turned out to be a kind man, easy-going, and rich and generous. And Pedro had learned that Mr. Taavi had studied at a school in Indiana, U. S. of A., and learned to build bridges there, which were things Pedro had never in his wildest moments ever dreamed he could do or learn, and so he had adjusted. He was even sad when, after he'd been employed for only a few months, Mr. Clint received a phone call to tell him Mr. Taavi had been killed while trying to build a bridge in Kentucky, U. S. of A. However, he also felt that a certain right order had been restored now that there was not a Mayan standing over him. Mr. Taavi's death confirmed his own conviction that safety in this world was not an attainable thing no matter how much one learned, or how fancy a job one had. Indeed, there was always the possibility that Mr. Taavi was dead because he was not content with his place in the world, because he was a Mayan who thought he was worthy of such a grand occupation – building bridges!

There was always the possibility, too, that Mr. Taavi was dead because he shared Mr. Clint's bedroom. This arrangement Pedro had always felt uncomfortably intrigued about, and if someone had to die for the sins that took place in that room, he was glad it was the Mayan. Mr. Clint was such a nice, blonde, American rich man; it would have been a shame if he had been the one who had to pay the price for the sins.

Pedro's people were farm hands and factory workers. As far back as a hundred and fifty years ago, the men in his family had worked in the fields, harvesting *Agave fourcroydes*, and in the mills producing the twine and rope from the *henequen*, the strong fibers that were derived from the agave plants. In those days, Merida had been home to more millionaires than anywhere else on Earth. It was the *henequen* barons who built these palaces on the *Paseo de Montejo*, and laid down the city's cobblestone streets, and erected its palm-shaded plazas. It had been the women in Pedro's family who had cleaned and cooked in those palaces, raised the children who lived in them, swept the streets and scrubbed the marble steps before them. Between the fields and the mills, and the kitchens and the nurseries, the people in families like Pedro's were able to make good livings and good lives, and, rich and poor, the people of Merida were happy. Or, at least, they were happy in their allotted places, all with food to eat and warm, dry places to sleep.

And then came the invention of artificial twine. Soon enough the millionaires were gone, along with the jobs that came with working at their factories and cleaning their homes, and their homes were abandoned and fell to ruin. This was all before Pedro was even born, of course, but his mother, a quiet lady prone to melancholy moods, would sometimes take him by the hand and walk him along the *Paseo de Montejo* and tell him stories of how it used to be long ago: This broad boulevard had been compared to the Champs Elysees! Pedro had never seen the Champs Elysees, of course, and he had no idea what his mother was talking about, but he'd seen photographs in school of a place in the U. S. of A. called Los Angeles, a city of angels, all the movie stars houses bright white and yellow and pink, all the streets lined with palm trees for shade from the burnishing sun, and he thought this must be what the Champs Elysees looked like, and he longed to the point of aching for such brilliance in his life.

Money was the thing that assured one had brilliance in his life. This much he knew for sure. And so, when he was a nine-year-old boy, and he was offered five American dollars to deliver a small if heavy box wrapped up in wrinkled brown paper from the *pulperia* near his neighborhood in Merida to a warehouse on the outskirts of town, he said he would do this. And, the next day, when he was offered ten American dollars to haul a small but heavy backpack to a hacienda four miles outside of Merida, he said he would do this too. At his destination he was rewarded with not only the ten dollars but most of a bottle of American lemonade and half of a thick ham sandwich that one of the armed men outside the hacienda didn't want to finish. Pedro had made his way back to his neighborhood feeling full and thinking that he had just been at the home of some very important rich guy. Who else but an important, rich guy would have men with guns to protect him?

The next day Pedro was offered a real pay day – twenty American dollars to go back to the warehouse where he'd delivered the original package and help to unload a big truck. The work was very hard. First he had to climb up in the big truck and lift a twenty-pound sack on his shoulder, and then he had to climb down out of the truck and haul the sack across two empty bays and down into a hatch in the floor and then stack the sack neatly onto the ever-taller stacks of sacks he was piling up. The three armed men who were guarding the truck – presumably for the important, rich guy whose hacienda he had visited just yesterday – didn't help him with the unloading. He wondered if maybe they were supposed to be helping him, but they only stood around, their guns on their backs, urging him to go faster on his skinny legs, laughing as he stumbled and grunted, but obeyed, and Pedro didn't complain because they gave him more lemonade, and shared their pork tacos with him – as many as he wanted. It was very hard work; he ate four tacos over the course of the day and all the armed men did was laugh and say he was going to fatten up if ate so much, or maybe he had a hollow leg and that was why he was able to eat so much and stay so small.

He was sore and it was dark by the time he returned home, but he had a full belly and twenty dollars American in his pocket. He gave his mother half his earnings – in secret; his father was a jolly man and if he had seen the money he would have said they should have meat for dinner and then his parents would have argued, his mother finally in tears and unable to eat at all, crying long after the meat was gone that his father had bought the family one meal when they could have had beans for three days. And so he went to bed happy.

The next day he wasn't so sore and he walked back to the warehouse to see if anyone was around and if they might have another job for him. The three armed men were there and they laughed when they saw him, and called him *chico flaco*, a name he was unfortunately used to, and fed him beef and cheese *huaraches*. They said there was no work that day, but come back tomorrow and maybe they would find something for him to do. And so he had gone back the next day and they had a job for him, standing on a corner near a *lavanderia* in a neighborhood near the *Paseo de Montejo,* handing out palm-sized, folded-paper parcels to anyone who handed him fifty American dollars in return.

"But…" Pedro nodded, "who will I give them to?"

One of the armed men shook his head. "The people who you will give them to will know who you are. They will ask you if you have anything for them and you will say, 'Yes, for fifty Americans,' and they will give you this money or you will not give them a piece of the paper. *Si?*"

"*Sí.*"

"All right," the man said and handed him a fistful of the parcels. "Don't come back until these are all gone. And when you do come back, you bring all the money here. Don't think to cheat, *chico flaco.*"

Pedro had shaken his head violently at the very idea; he would not say he didn't know what he had agreed to do. That he didn't know what trade he was plying. "How much will you give me when I come back with all the money?"

The armed man laughed. "How much do you want?"

Pedro was at a loss. How much he wanted and what was proper to ask for were, perhaps, not the same thing.

"Thirty dollars," the man told him. "Will that make you happy?"

Pedro thought of his mother's face when he would hand her half of this sum this very evening, and he giggled so hard he made the armed men laugh again.

"Where are you getting all this money?" his mother asked.

"Sweeping the steps at some of the shops before they open in the morning," Pedro lied. Lying to his mother made him feel as cold as her smiling face made him happy.

"Who pays a little boy fifteen American dollars to sweep some steps?"

"And I wash the shop windows, and take sacks of flour off trucks and stack them in the shop basements too."

Pedro's mother was frowning, but nodding too, convinced because she wanted to be. "Just don't be late for dinner. Your father likes all the family around the table to eat. Tonight, maybe a little meat, to make your father happy," she said. "How would you like that?"

Pedro had saved one hundred and ninety-five dollars, half of all his earnings, and his family had had meat for many meals, before his job on the corner by the *lavande-ria* came to an end. He went to the warehouse late one afternoon to turn in the day's revenues and collect his thirty Americans, and he saw that the three armed men who were his employers had been disarmed. They were on the other end of guns held now by twice as many armed men who stood around in a semi-circle; of the three unarmed men, two of them were standing behind a table piled high with *pan dulce* growing stale, and one of the them was sitting on a chair with his eyes squinted closed, sweat dripping on his face, holding his leg over a puddle of blood on the concrete floor. Pedro saw what looked to him like a big, white tooth poking out from a ragged hole in the man's dark blue velour jogging pants. One more man, an older man who was wearing a shining white linen blazer draped over his shoulders, stood inside of the circle. "Who are you?" the older man bellowed when Pedro let himself inside the warehouse door.

Pedro wanted to run back out the door, but his legs felt flimsy, and he saw one of the six men in the semi-circle turn his gun casually to point at him.

"I say, *who are you*?" the older man insisted, but Pedro was unable to speak, which made the older man snort. "The little errand boy, I think? The one who has been selling the wares these *ladrones* have stolen from me!"

Pedro thought it was best not to try to fool the man who seemed to be in control of where the guns were pointing. He still couldn't speak, but he reached into his pocket and handed the older man the wad of five hundred American dollars he had collected that day.

The older man grunted, and gestured for one of his gunman to take the money from the boy. "How much do they pay you to steal from me?"

Pedro wanted so much to speak. To shout, *I didn't steal from you*. What he choked out was, "Thirty dollars – "

The older man seemed to find this amusing. He clapped his hands together and laughed and turned to the three unarmed men. "You steal not only from me, but from this little boy!" Then he gestured to the gunman again, who counted out thirty dollars from the wad in his hand and handed it to Pedro. The older man waited until Pedro had the three ten-dollar bills wadded in his sweating fist before he spoke again. "Get out. Get out, little man, and you never come here again. You do not remember where you have been or you will share the fate of these stupid men who steal from me – "

Pedro saw the eyes of the wounded man in the chair open, and grow wide, and wet. He heard one of the standing men, the one who had made the deal with him and given him this fine job, say, "It was only a little, a *pinch*, from just a few of the big sacks, and we will give you this money, Pablo – " before he was running and out the door and taking himself far away but not far enough away that he didn't hear the *rat-a-tat-tat* of six AK-47s.

Pedro's mother took the fifteen American dollars her son handed to her and did not ask why when he told her to spend it wisely as it was all he had. He put his share of the day's profit under the mattress with his other savings. Two hundred and ten dollars. He had sprawled in his bed just this morning adding up how much he would have in just two more weeks on the job, and then at the end of the month, and then how much he would have at the end of two months, and then how much he would have at the end of six months of this work. Just this morning it seemed to him that he had been on the verge of undreamed-of riches.

Instead he went back to school, and tried to do well at his studies, which was frustrating for him as he was not by nature a happy student. He came home after school and dutifully did his homework, and he helped his mother to prepare meals that were poor again without his contributions to the grocery fund. He sometimes would go outside in the evenings, after dinner, and watch his friends play ball in the street, though he did not often feel like playing himself. He preferred to stay inside, helping his mother wash up after dinner, or untangling the threads in her sewing basket, or ironing his father's shirts so she could have a rest in the evenings because she didn't have to do it herself. He never found occasion to return to the part of town where the warehouse had been located, and he never spoke to anyone of his ordeal. He simply found it hard to be a child again.

Then he had seen it begin, the old Americans coming with their money to Merida. Buying the old colonial houses on and around the *Paseo de Montejo*, painting them bright white, tending to the neglected palms, repairing the cobblestones, restoring the plazas. A job in any one of those houses would have been an opportunity his father liked to call "golden". His father was working steadily once more, tending the lawns of the rich gringos, and his mother had found a place cleaning in their big houses four days a week, and his older brothers, though not skilled, found work on the crews that were restoring the palaces. Pedro, though, had been the luckiest of all his family. He had found a job with Clint Kennedy, who was still a young man, only ten or fifteen years his elder, and handsome, kind, generous. Mr. Clint's house felt like some kind of safety, even if it meant that Pedro must call a Mayan *Mr. Taavi*. And then, soon enough Mr. Taavi was dead and Pedro's job was perfect.

Pedro did not like to sweep, or dust, and it was fortunate that Mr. Clint was not as particular about such things as Pedro's mother was, but he did like to polish Mr. Clint's silver candleholders, and to keep the water in the pool on his patio sparkling blue, and to cook him the Mexican food that he enjoyed so much. And Pedro loved to do laundry, to press fine crisp seams into the linen shirts Mr. Clint liked to wear, and to polish his leather sandals, and to pack his bag when he took his increasingly frequent trips to Miami.

In the last months, it seemed to Pedro that Mr. Clint took one of these trips, often just overnight, at least once a week. He began to have people over to his house late at night – his banker, he told Pedro. He began to invite guests from America to visit and took them to a bullfight in which the matador was the notorious Alvaro Moreno. He began to put more and more of his money into that school he had started for Mayan kids, of all people, and Pedro had begun to feel unsettled about that. Jealous. Why couldn't normal Mexican boys go to Mr. Clint's fancy *academia*? Pedro had begun to feel unsafe. He could not put his finger on any particular reason for this feeling, but there it was. And then one day, when Mr. Clint was lounging by his pool, the very Alvaro Moreno himself came marching into Mr. Clint's home with many of his men and they hauled Mr. Clint away.

That was when Pedro first spoke to his melancholy mother about his fears. "A place to live, and all the food you can eat, and three hundred American dollars a week – you will not find another job like this again," she warned. He spoke to his jolly father. "And how did you think your young American was making so much money anyway? Do you think even young American men make money like that when they are not involved with people like Alvaro Moreno?" He laughed at his son. Pedro's older brothers laughed too, when their father spoke of Pedro's naivety over the dinner table that very night. "*Chico flaco*," they teased. "*Chico flaco cobarde*. This is what you still are. This is what you will always be!"

But then, now, just this afternoon, another man had marched into Mr. Clint's house. It was the older man from the warehouse, who did not seem to recognize Pedro who, after all, was grown now and no longer a little boy. "Mr. Clint," the older man said, "is going to be away for a while. I will be taking over his house while he is gone, using it for my business associates when they come to town. It will make a fine place for them to stay. Clint has always spoken highly of you – what is your name?"

"Pedro."

"Yes, yes. Pedro. He has always told me this house boy of his is quite good at his job, so you're welcome to stay on, if you'd like. I'll match whatever Clint was paying you, of course…"

The older man kept talking. Pedro nodded as he spoke, wiped his sweating palms on the sides of his trousers, and thought that it was time to return to his mother's house, and to ironing his father's shirts. It was time again to seek safety elsewhere.

ASILAH

Morocco, 2010

Casablanca, Marrakesh, Tangier – these would have been the obvious choices. I picked Asilah mostly because I couldn't stand to become a cliché, but also because it is a genuinely beautiful city. I would recommend it even to those not in hiding from the law.

I thought I could feel at home in Asilah, and that had a lot to do with its similarities to Merida, my Yucatan paradise, the White City. As in Merida, the predominate color of the buildings is a blindingly beautiful white and, as in Merida, the streets are rigorously swept and washed down, and litter free. Happily, Moroccans are generally as hospitable and easy-going as Mexicans and that was another similarity I greatly appreciated, though the language barrier was a much greater obstacle to friendship. I spoke enough Spanish to get by in Mexico; I spoke not one word of Berber when I arrived in Asilah.

"Nous nous?" Kamal asked, though he didn't have to: I began nearly every day with what was, essentially, a Moroccan latte. Kamal was the owner of the café nearest to the apartment I rented in Asilah. He was usually just opening up when I began my day – not that I slept late but in Morocco the people don't typically start their day with coffee; it's more of a mid-morning treat and there was no call for him to open at the crack of dawn as he would have had to in America. "What is it I should call it again?"

Kamal spoke better-than-average English, but he could never remember the word *regular*. "Regular, Kamal. It's my *regular* drink."

"Your *regular*?" he repeated, slowly, trying once again to memorize it. Sometimes he'd ask if I wanted my regulation, or my recommend, or my rectum, which always cracked me up.

I began my days at around eight in the morning. I'd write in my journal for half an hour or so, recording the particulars of my time in exile and, when I was done, lock the book away in a small, pad-locked, fire-proof box I kept under my bed. Then I'd leave my apartment, small and sparse but with the requisite oriel windows that overlooked the Atlantic, stop at Kamal's for my regular nous nous and a little conversation, and head out for a run along the coast.

Asilah was a fortified city at the northwest tip of Morocco; its medieval ramparts are still intact and it was a kick for someone like me, who loved the architecture of historic structures, to run every morning by walls that had been barricades during the Portuguese crusades in 1578, and harbored pirates in the 1800s. Indeed, Asilah had existed since 1500 BC, and I found little pieces of history everywhere – the ancient Kasbah, and the still-lively Medina – though I was gratified that the whole city had undergone a renovation in the last thirty years or so; all the charm of an ageless city with all the modern conveniences.

"Your regular, Mr. Kennedy?" Kamal said again.

I thought he was practicing the word, but I answered, "Very good, as always."

"What I want to tell you is your regular is a woman's drink."

I frowned at my tall glass of coffee like I was looking for – what? A little pink paper umbrella?

"Men do not *generally* take milk with their coffee," Kamal advised.

I smiled, but I also rolled my eyes heavenward. Moroccans were – *generally* – very particular about gender divides, but I did not think I could get used to drinking their syrupy thick espresso straight every morning.

"I have five unsolved murders," Detective Louis Aiello said, "and there are threads to Clint Kennedy in each and every one of them." He leaned against the ornate brass Art Deco elevator doors of the Miami-Dade County courthouse, stalling, and enumerated: "The dead lawyer out on Okeechobee Road, the dead pilot *and* the dead gardener in Little Havana, the two thugs we found dead in the Everglades – ”

"*Threads…*" the D.A. repeated. "And that means all you have is circumstantial evidence, Lou. You can't *tie* him to anything." He tried to reach around the detective, to the panel of buttons on the wall so he could call for an elevator, but Lou Aiello pushed himself off the doors to block him. He towered over the tiny D.A.

"His house in Merida – not to mention that school he started down there – have been taken over by Pablo Navarro. How did his property end up in the hands of a notorious drug lord if he's not involved with the guy? Why is he not to be found in either of his homes, Miami or Merida, if he's so goddamned clean?"

"I'm not saying he's clean, Lou, I'm saying you don't have anything you can pin on him." He stepped around the detective and jabbed the button for his floor.

"I would if you'd get me a warrant to tap the Cohens' phones. My gut tells me he's in contact with that family."

"So, you want me to go to a judge and tell him to issue a warrant based on your gut?" The D.A. chuckled. He was nearly fifty, short and broad and balding, but not without a sense of humor. The elevator dinged its arrival and the D.A. backed into it, pointing a finger at the detective, still smiling. "You're going to have to come up with something better than that if you'd like to tap the phones of David and Candace Cohen."

Asilah is about twenty miles south of Tangier. I could have run the whole way there on the coast road – and probably should have; Moroccan food is delicious and, in spite of daily runs, I'd gained over five pounds since I'd been in the country – but the day was growing hot. It was September, past the peak heat of summer, but unless I wanted to start my runs at six AM, five miles was all I was going to be able to put in until more wintery weather set in.

Besides, it was Thursday: market day. I wanted to hit the stalls early, before the tourists descended. Asilah was also past the peak of the July/August tourist season, and the next big invasion wouldn't happen until the skiers arrived in January, but the city's main modern industry is tourism, and it's a year-round venture. The influx might slow from season-to-season, but it never really stops. It was one of the things that made me want to settle here: a steady stream of Americans coming to visit; I would not stand out.

I stopped by my apartment for a shower before I headed to the market, kicking off my running shoes outside my front door. It was a custom here in Morocco, to remove one's shoes before entering a home, and it was a custom I took to instantly. I liked the cleanliness of it and, I thought, if I ever made it back home, it was one I'd import.

Modesty is also a custom in Morocco – not so much in the cities as in the rural areas, but not even the tourists walked around in short-shorts and tank tops on these streets. Not many women wore veils – headscarves were the covering of choice for the vast majority and, in the few conversations I'd had with the natives in my brief time here, my understanding of *why* they wore them had evolved. In a culture where female virginity is highly prized – and the loss of it sometimes brutally punished – women think of their head coverings as a sort of armor against unwanted attentions. I had seen more than one quite sophisticated-looking woman draw her scarf around her face when she'd become the subject of unsolicited notice, and the man had backed off nearly instantaneously. That sort of retreat is also a cultural wonder, of course – I could imagine the subtlety of the woman's gesture being lost on some lout in an American sports bar – but here, in Morocco, it would work on all but the most determined criminal.

I had also, for the record, seen any number of Moroccan sex workers covered from head to toe, their faces thoroughly obscured with heavy veils, all in the service of disguising their trade. It worked both ways.

Modesty also applies to men, which I shouldn't have been surprised to discover, but I was. We fellows are expected to cover ourselves from our shoulders to below the knee, though this is not strictly enforced except in the more rural areas of the country. In order to be respectful to the local customs, I had taken to wearing a sort of a uniform: a chambray dress shirt with sleeves rolled to just above the wrist, and baggy, colorful board shorts that hit just below the knee. I don't suppose in my wildest imaginings there would have been any other circumstance under which I would have donned a pair of board shorts, but clothing that was, as the fashion industry puts it, *body con*, would have gotten me a lot of side-eye looks, and board shorts were cut wide. I had found a brand I liked and Candace had sent several packages of them to Kamal's café for me in the few months I'd been in exile.

The days are hot this time of year in Morocco, but the nights get damned cold. I'd taken to wrapping a bright, long, linen scarf a couple of times around my neck whenever I went out, so I'd always have one handy if I ended up staying out later than I'd planned. I finished off with suede Birkenstock sandals, a pair of retro aviator Ray-Bans, and an embossed burnt-orange Moroccan leather fanny pack into which I tucked my wallet, my keys, and a large canvas shopping bag, and headed out to market.

"It's not as if he's being especially discreet," the D.A. said.

Judge Errol Kushner raised an eyebrow. "How so?"

The D.A. usually enjoyed meeting the judge in his courthouse office, sinking into the deep leather upholstery of the chair before the judge's desk, the cocoon of the antique polished walnut paneling on the walls. But, Christ, this Clint Kennedy the judge had asked about was leaving himself wide open.

"Look, Errol," the D. A. said, "I didn't want to raise any red flags, so I hired a P.I. I work with sometimes, off the record, you know, and it took him less than forty-eight hours to find out Candace Cohen has been sending packages to a coffeeshop in a city called Asilah, in Morocco. Why would she be doing that? Who does she know in Morocco? Clint Kennedy? Occam's razor, man."

The judge bent his head and rubbed his brow.

"I mean, where else would he go?" the D.A. added. "Only a place where there's no extradition, of course. It doesn't help me think Kennedy's innocent when he runs off to a place where there's no extradition."

The judge nodded – not to confirm Clint's where-abouts, he was purposely not privy to that information, but in understanding of the D.A.'s reasoning. "What about that detective? Aiello?"

The D.A. grunted. "He's got nothing. Nothing but a lot of conjecture. Even if the request for a warrant to tap the Cohens doesn't come before you, no judge is going to sign off on it the way it reads now."

Kushner let himself feel a moment of relief. A split second of it. "Unless Aiello finds out about the packages going to – Where did you say?"

"Asilah."

"Asilah. Yes."

The D.A. shrugged. "Would you sign off even in that case?"

Kushner shook his head.

"Right. But, I'll tell you, Errol, this Aiello is a fucking terrier. He's got a bone and he's shaking it. I know you want your boy left alone, but if Aiello comes up with something that looks like it'll stick, I can't run interference."

The judge looked up at the D.A. and said, "*Of course not*," as if he meant it.

I picked up a tomato and brought it to my nose. Was there anything better than the smell of a sun-warmed tomato? I already had a lot of the ingredients I needed to make the vegetable tagine I wanted to prepare for myself that evening – including, of course, a big, proper, bright blue clay pot I'd bought at the souk when I'd first arrived. I needed a big pot for this endeavor. As I ran at least five miles every morning, my weight gain wasn't due to inactivity but from eating out every night. Asilah is a city awash in restaurants that are so much more than merely decent, and I adore Moroccan food. As, however, I had always been a competent if reluctant cook, now was the time to hone my rusty skills and put them to use. I planned on making enough tagine to keep myself out of the restaurants for a good three or four days.

I had the necessary onions and garlic, carrots and potatoes in the small pantry in my apartment. I needed to pick up some dried apricots, which would give that subtle, Moroccan sweetness to my vegetable stew, and some harissa, that deliciously aromatic blend of chili, caraway, fennel, and sumac, as well as cinnamon, coriander, and turmeric that give a tagine its characteristic warmth and intensity. Of all the stalls in the crowded, invigorating crush of the souk, the spice vendor's was my very favorite. I made my way toward it slowly, like a kid who waits to open his big present on Christmas morning until after he's opened all the packages of new socks and underwear.

Meantime, I needed tomatoes, half a dozen or so. I picked up another one, held it to my nose, and inhaled. It wasn't the scent of the tomato that provoked my next thought, but the *voluptuousness* of the scent: My sex life sucks.

Opportunities for premarital sex, of either the casual or the more committed variety, with women were few and far between – reference my previous remarks about the cultural importance of female purity – and homosexuality is illegal in Morocco. I did not succumb to traditional gender roles, dictated here by law and religion; rather, my *need* to defy those traditional roles in any way was not a burning one. When Taavi had been killed, I'd entered into a period of voluntary celibacy ordained by grief. I wondered now if abstinence had become mere habit? A bad habit, surely, and one I would willingly have broken if the appropriate occasion had presented itself. I simply found myself uninspired about orchestrating such an occasion. I'd approached some of the veiled sex work-

ers on one darkened street or another, but any interest
that had propelled the approach invariably faded upon
engagement; I ended up thanking the woman, often rudi-
mentally, working around whatever language she spoke,
handing off a couple of dirham notes to compensate her
for her time, and fleeing in relief. I'd paged through a
couple issues of *Mithly*, the magazine produced by Kif-
Kif, the country's LGBTQ organization – and printed in
Spain to get around the fact that the publication was not
officially permitted in Morocco – but I could read the
language no better than I could speak it. What I knew
for sure was that the penalty for homosexuality here was
a hefty fine and up to three years in jail. The threat of a
fine didn't bother me – I was well provided for – but I had
already done time. Twice. And I had no desire to do it
ever again. I could describe in detail the conditions in the
prisons of two countries – the United States and Mexico
– and I did not want to find out what the conditions were
like in a Moroccan jail.

Or, maybe, my lack of want for even minimal carnal
gratification was a product of being on the lam. You may
read these words and believe I was leading a luxurious
and leisurely life in Asilah but, let me assure you, the
pressures involved in evading the American police in a
foreign country cut close to a man's bones on an hourly
basis. *Was that man following me? Wasn't he there the last
time I was in this restaurant too? Is that woman looking at
me? Why is she looking at me!* I didn't want to compound

the stress so I was not merely practicing discretion, I was hunkered down well below the radar.

I picked up another warm, voluptuous tomato and did not allow myself to sniff it before I added it to my canvas shopping bag.

David Cohen sat at the desk in his office at his estate in Homestead. More recently than he cared to remember he'd suffered a stroke, while on an extended vacation with his wife in the Bahamas. While he was recovering to everyone's satisfaction – including, he supposed, his own – he was restless. His doctor had told him it would be another four to six months until he could take to the tennis court again, and the few laps he was allowed in the pool every morning for exercise were not enough to burn off what he considered a healthy amount of energy. Or his frustration. And Candace, the wife he adored, was a damned prison warden about making sure he stayed well within the parameters his doctor had dictated – exercise, diet. Sex.

At least she had released him from his wheelchair. The pleasure of sitting behind his desk in his actual desk chair – leather, in a design much more ergonomically-friendly than even the fanciest wheelchair could hope to mimic – was not to be underestimated. He swiveled his chair so he could reach the bottom right-hand drawer of his desk and unlock it with the key he kept innocuously among the bits and bobs in a crystal ashtray on his desk – an ashtray that would, according to Candace, never again see the butt of one of the Marlboros she'd heretofore pretended he did not smoke. The key turned smoothly and David pulled a brown leather ledger from within.

David, a banker, was by nature meticulous with his accounts. He was not, however, used to keeping what amounted to two sets of books, let alone in code, but now that he was responsible for Clint's money, this was required.

The businesses that Clint had founded – or invested in, such as the Cohen family bank – before he'd had to flee were thriving. This, David was proud to say, was the result of the excellence with which his son, Jack, was managing those businesses in Clint's absence, though there lingered the possibility that legal trouble would come for Clint and certain assets would be frozen. Or even confiscated. Hence the necessity for the dual and coded bookkeeping system David had devised, along with, of course, a little shuffling of the names on owner-ship documents. This was for Clint's benefit as well as for the benefit of the Cohen family – they'd all be up a creek if it wasn't only Clint's assets that ended up frozen and none of them had access to cash. David was scrupulous about recording Clint's share of all profits, and transfer-ring portions of those funds on both a regular and an as-needed basis to Clint, via Switzerland.

"Darling?" Candace rapped on his office door.

"Yes, dear?"

"Well, you'll be so pleased to hear, Errol Kushner has stopped by to see us."

David froze, but only for an instant. He quickly, quietly closed the ledger before him and dropped it the bottom desk drawer, all the while chuckling, drawing out his reply, "Oh, well, yes, isn't that a nice surprise then? Yes, dear, will you show the judge in, please?"

David had just returned the key to the crystal ashtray as Candace cracked the door and allowed Errol Kushner to enter. "So very good to see you, Errol," David said, extending his hand. "Forgive me if I don't get up."

Errol took the hand offered to him. "Of course, please don't," he replied.

David was certainly well able to get to his feet to greet a visitor by this point in his recovery, but not beneath using his recent illness as an excuse not to rise for those he deemed unworthy of the effort. "Have a seat, Errol," he said, gesturing to the chair before his desk. "What brings you here today?"

Errol Kushner was as uncomfortable in David's home office as David was having him there. "I'll get right to the point."

"Please do."

"First thing, you have to tell your damned wife to stop sending packages to Clint. It's too fucking easy to follow her trail right to him, should anyone decide to want to do that."

What a stunning thing to say, David thought. Not that the idea his wife was sending care packages to a young man she adored as a third son surprised him at all – it was in Candace's nature to take care of those she loved – but that Kushner had had the balls to modify the word *wife* with an adjective like *damned*. And in reference to Candace! David took a deep breath. There would be no benefit in calling out the judge on this lack of judgment in this matter; better just to chalk it up to the fact that Kushner had made the mistake of marrying young and to a miserable woman. He was clearly laboring under the misguided premise that all marriages were as sour as his own.

"And the second thing, Errol?" David asked.

"Aiello is a dog with a bone. He's not going to let this go. He wants Clint for questioning at the very least, and I can't guarantee how much longer the D. A. is going to be willing to play along."

The tagine smelled heavenly, though it still had four hours to stew before I could eat it. I despaired, momentarily, of ever reclaiming my prior weight while living in a land with food this tempting: roast chicken with preserved lemons and olives; lamb stew seasoned with saffron and ginger, finished with prunes and crunchy almonds; rfissa, which is a stewed chicken with lentils, seasoned with fenugreek, and is, as I discovered early in my residence in Morocco, the mother of all comfort foods. Harira, and mechoui and sardines stuffed with a marinade of chermoula and served whole! Even my beloved Mexican delicacies had nothing on this stuff.

I sighed and pulled a bottle of rare Moroccan white wine from my refrigerator – rare because, while the Moroccan wine industry is a high-growth enterprise, the climate is best suited to red varietals; only three per-cent of their wines are white and that is rather a shame as some of them are quite good. The one I opened that afternoon was a Clairette blanche, a traditional grape for the region that produces a highly drinkable, high-alco-hol wine that, unfortunately, tends to oxidize quickly; once you take out the cork you commit to the bottle, so I knew what I was going to be doing for the rest of the day while the tagine cooked.

I took a wine glass, the bottle of white wine in a clay cooler, and my current book out to my balcony. *The Girl Who Kicked the Hornets' Nest* was the book everyone was reading that year and I was too, though my big plan for while I was in exile was to read all the greats I'd hereto-fore been too busy to crack. My first wish list consisted of reading at least one work from every Nobel laureate in literature from 1901 onward. I had decided to start at the beginning, with the first winner of the prize, Sully Prudhomme, and was initially discouraged when I found out he wrote in French, which I neither read nor speak. I wondered if this was a sign, from God or Taavi, that I ought to learn that language, but I grew even gloomier when I realized how rigorous such study would be. Then Kamal offered to let me borrow his computer, and I logged onto his Internet connection and found a book of Prudhomme's poems in translation.

The décor in my apartment consists mainly of all the books I'd bought on the days I'd borrowed Kamal's laptop. Books and a bed, a lounge chair for my balcony and the bright blue tagine. For security reasons I had no laptop of my own, no tablet; only a burner phone I discarded and replaced with regularity. Working forward through the list, I'd made it to Rudyard Kipling, 1907 – and I might have made it even further but for Stieg Larsson captivating everyone that season. Still, I wasn't hard on myself for the pace I was keeping; I was a fugitive: what else did I have to do except improve myself?

There was the softest breeze on my balcony, stifling heat tempered with what felt like waves of cool blowing in from the Atlantic that spread out blue and vast below me. I poured the wine, propped myself up on the lounge chair, and cracked my book.

I must have been reading for about an hour when I heard the first footstep. I actually wondered, for a moment, if it was my already vivid imagination under the influence of Larsson that had put me on edge, so I put the book down and listened more closely –

No. That was definitely another footstep I'd just heard.

My apartment is actually the top floor of a house: two rooms, a bath, and a rudimentary kitchen set up against one of the walls in the room I use as a living room. The main house takes up the first two floors – which is occupied by the owners of the property, a youngish family consisting of an attorney named Yousef, his wife, Zahra, who is an historian currently working on a book about the hundred-year Portuguese occupation of Morocco that started in the year 1415, and their two little girls, ages seven and nine. My apartment is on the third floor and completely separated from Yousef and Zahra's residence, accessed by a steep, white staircase at one side of the house that leads to a sort of vertical half-wall into which my front door is set. The door opens directly onto my balcony. Usually, during a weekday, I can count on being alone in the building – Yousef being at his law offices, Zahra at the library doing research, and the little girls at school.

I heard the third footstep, flattened myself against the lounge chair and peered at the half-wall. It affords all the privacy in the world, unless someone decides to come up to the top of my staircase, stand on their toes and bend uncomfortably to the right. Then my whole balcony – including me, rigid in the lounger – would be on view. *Is this how it ends*, I thought? *Captured on a sunny afternoon made to be spent with strong wine and a captivating book?*

I heard three more quick footsteps, making their way toward me, and I chanced sitting up and looking over the wall of my balcony to the street below, which was quiet, as usual. A pair of older ladies walking by, their shopping bags a clue that they were on their way to market, but no traffic. No cars or, importantly, police cars. And, surely, if I was going to be picked up by the authorities, the word would have gotten through the Miami-Dade County grapevine and Jack would have gotten word to me to clear out –

There were six more quick footsteps that stopped just at the half-wall, and then three solid raps on the door that led inside, to me. I sat up, ramrod straight in the lounger, my heart beating as fast as my quick, shallow breaths. *There is no extradition from Morocco*, I repeated, possibly out loud, like a mantra. And then I heard, "Clint? Clint! Are you there?"

"Jesus Christ."

I heard laughter. "No, Yousef."

I flung open the door. "What are you doing home at this hour?"

Yousef was holding his tasseled loafers in one hand, so polite he wouldn't even walk shod up my stairs. That he'd stopped to remove them on his way up explained the unsteady rhythm of his footsteps.

"We had a leak this morning," he said.

"Oh, I'm sorry – " I panted, though my breathing was returning to normal.

He waved a hand to wave away my sympathies. "I am the one who is sorry. We were able to shut down the water to only our bathroom when it happened, but now the plumber is here and I must shut down the water in the whole house. I came to tell you to draw drinking water now as the plumber thinks it will be possibly tomorrow until we can turn it back on."

"Bad leak then?"

"I was in the shower and the wall in front of me crumbled. I had to finish washing in the kitchen sink."

"You should have called me – I would have waited on the plumber for you."

"Thank you, but I wouldn't disturb you. And I am already here, and I've brought some work home to occupy me."

"But, your girls…"

"Zahra's on a deadline for her publisher, so her father will pick them up and bring them home after school."

I nodded. "Really, though. If you need anything."

"Thank you, Clint," he said, but he was already making his way back down the stairs.

"My pleasure," I mumbled as I closed the door behind him. This is the worst part of being in exile, I thought: You don't know anyone well enough for them to feel comfortable disturbing you. Even when their bathroom wall crumbles before them. And that meant you knew no one well enough to tell them you are living in fear, waiting for the footfalls, the knock, that will take you down. I could put on a show that would con the whole world, but the truth is I am homesick as fuck

– and admitting it now, even just to myself, made me feel that I might not have to cry after all. So far, I had avoided that step into real depression.

Jack Cohen pulled into his parents' circular drive and cut the engine while he finished his conversation with Rudy, his boyfriend of nearly seven months. Jack had never dated anyone for such a long stretch, and he'd certainly never tried living with another human being before – not since he'd left his parents' house for college – and he, himself, was shocked to find that he absolutely loved it. Loved everything about it, even the way Rudy, a dress designer, went on about things like the gorgeous chartreuse silk shantung that had just been delivered to his atelier that morning, or the recipe for the curried egg salad he'd made for lunch.

"How late are you going to be? I've got a couple strips, quick meal, I'm exhausted, been sewing silk georgette all day and that shit's a bitch to work with, just call me when you're on the way and I'll fire the grill – "

Jack smiled. Ordinarily, chatter of this order would have made him feel hemmed in, controlled – *What if I don't want steak for dinner? What then? And I'll stay at my parents' house as long as I want to stay,* he could imagine himself snapping at any other of the multitude of guys he'd dated over the course of his thirty-five years. Perhaps the key this time was that he knew that if he ever said anything like that to Rudy, Rudy would simply pop one of the steaks in the freezer and tell Jack not to wake him when he got in. Jack couldn't wait to get home, but he clicked off his phone and unbuckled his seatbelt and headed into his parents' house – *ever the dutiful son*, he smiled.

"Darling!" Candace called when he walked into the kitchen. "Rudy's not with you?"

Jack kissed her and gave her an extra squeeze, so she giggled when he hugged her. "He's at home, making me dinner."

Candace grinned. "Then you ought to be home too."

"Soon enough. Where's Dad?"

Jack knocked on his father's office door.

"Yes?"

"Just me, Dad," Jack called, and David didn't bother putting the ledger away again.

"Have you spoken with Clint lately?" David asked when Jack had taken a seat in front of his desk.

Jack shrugged. "Maybe a couple of weeks ago. Erring on the side of caution. But I miss him, you know?"

David nodded. He did know. But there were other, bigger considerations this evening. "Listen, Jack," he said.

So Jack did. Then he went out to the kitchen and kissed his mother goodbye, climbed into his car, buckled himself in, and pulled a burner phone out of the glove compartment.

He didn't call Pablo often – only when necessary; but with Clint out of the picture for the foreseeable future, Jack was the one running his businesses on a day-to-day basis, interfacing with Clint's Mexican banker, and Clint's assistant, Tim, and, ultimately, Pablo, when the occasion called for it. He always felt light-headed as he dialed Pablo's number, and was always surprised at how patiently Pablo listened to whatever he had to say. How reasoned his responses always were.

"It seems to me," Pablo said when Jack had finished talking, "that we have two options. First, we could make sure this Detective Aiello doesn't go digging any deeper into our business."

Jack grunted. "I don't know what anyone would get on that guy. As far as I can tell, he's a straight arrow, a real family kind of guy – " He stopped when he realized what Pablo was suggesting. "No. No, Pablo. Please. What's option number two?"

Pablo sighed. "We could make sure your D.A. stays on the job."

That sounded more palatable. Staying *on the job* meant staying *alive* – that Pablo understood they were all better off with someone in the D.A.'s office who had proven he would work with them, versus some unknown quantity who'd let Aiello roam completely unfettered.

"Let's do that," Jack said. Pablo was quiet on the other end of the line, so Jack added, "The second thing. Let's do the second thing."

"For now," Pablo agreed. "But, we keep our options open."

Pablo disconnected the call, and Jack drove six miles out of the way, to a construction site off the Dolphin Expressway, where he put his car into park while he wiped his fingerprints off the burner before laying it on the ground and stomping it so it shattered and throwing it into a dumpster.

"Hi, honey," he called to Rudy when he finally opened his own front door. "I'm home."

I drew several large bowls full of water. I had a home fit for a fugitive – sparse; few things that would have to be left behind in flight save the tagine – and I had no other suitable vessels. I ate my dinner and finished my wine, scraped my plate into the trash can and left it in the sink to wash whenever the water came back on, annoyed I couldn't even rinse it. I realized that, if I'd given the water situation more thought, I would have borrowed a bucket from Yousef so I'd have some way of flushing the toilet while the plumbing was being repaired. As it was, I decided to take myself out to the little club I'd heard about near Paradise Beach. I could get a beer, listen to some music, and pee in a functional toilet.

There is no such thing as "Moroccan music". It varies greatly from region to region: Arabic music, such as the *aita* one hears on the Atlantic plains; the *melhoune* of the Andalusian cities; the Hassani of the Moroccan

Sahara, to name but a few. Moreover, young Moroccan musicians who have been influenced by music from all over the world will synthesize metal, blues, rap, rock with the spirit of the traditional music. The club near Paradise Beach that night was featuring a four-piece band channeling both reggae and the *ahidus* of the Middle Atlas, and they weren't bad.

I nursed a Casablanca beer at a table for two near the back of the club where it was darkest. Where the light from the stage that spilled generously to the dance floor didn't quite reach. I listened to the music, and to the voices around me of people I didn't know. Would probably never know, if only because the language barrier would keep us out of each other's lives. I heard Berber to my left, a tongue so far removed from my abilities that I didn't have the slightest clue what dialect the speakers were employing. To my right, I heard Darija, a dialect of Arabic and the most widely used language in Morocco; I had a few words in this language, mostly thanks to Kamal's attempts to teach me even as I corrected his English, but not enough that they would have allowed me to carry on a conversation. I heard a spattering of French, the language of business and commerce in Morocco and in which every student who finishes secondary school is fluent, but which I had opted out of studying, preferring to read the translated works of a long-dead poet to the possibility of actual human communication in the present. I heard no English that night, or even Spanish, in which I might have had a fighting chance of making myself understood to a potential dance partner.

I sipped my Casablanca. By the time I'd drained the glass I had resolved that self-pity was the scourge of the exile. Between the effects of the afternoon's wine that I was still feeling and, now, buoyed by the beer, this felt like a revelation. *Buck up*, I advised myself, threw a few dirhams on the table, and walked myself home.

The D.A. sat behind his desk in the room off the kitchen that had become his study when he and his wife bought this beach house over twenty years before. The plan had long been to remodel the house at some point – expand the kitchen and make what was now his home office into a breakfast room, build an addition behind the garage to serve as his study, and with a separate entrance. Between his career and his wife's, and with the arrival of each of the three kids, that plan had become merely a dream.

Still, the little room sufficed. And it had a majestic view of the Atlantic Ocean through a wall of glass windows in front of his desk; it comforted him that, in any case, he would have been hard-pressed to give up that view.

It was dark outside now, the scene before him speckled with lights from the stars above and the marina below. He hadn't turned on the lights when he'd arrived home – his wife and the kids were already asleep in their beds, and he didn't want to wake them. The light from the computer and its start-up *bing* seemed intrusive when he turned it on.

He swiveled in his desk chair, reached for the bottle of Johnny Walker Red he kept on the credenza, and poured himself a nightcap before he swiveled back to the computer screen and pulled up the schedule his secretary would have, as always, sent him for the following day. He'd taken his jacket off and hung it on the back of his desk chair before he'd sat down, and he reached behind him now, to retrieve the small, brown Moroccan leather notebook out of the breast pocket. His wife gave him half a dozen such notebooks for this birthday every year, each one embossed with his initials, in gold, on the front cover. He'd had a busy year and he was going to have to ask her to get him a couple more before he turned forty-nine.

He opened the email with his schedule in it, noted his next day's meetings and their times on a fresh page, and slipped the notebook back into the breast pocket. He was just about to turn off the computer, sit back and enjoy his scotch and the view, when he noticed a new, blue folder on the computer screen. "Huh," he said, and thought, *That's curious*, as he clicked to open it.

He looked with horror at the contents.

His first impulse was to erase it, dump it in the trash and then empty the trash, but he knew well enough that if anyone was looking for it they would find its digital trail.

His second impulse was to pick up the phone and alert his office that he had been hacked.

Strangely, given his profession, the question of who'd put the folder on his computer was only the third thought to enter his mind.

Then the landline rang. Instinctively he jumped to pick up the call, before the ringing woke his family.

"If you tell someone what is on your computer," said the man on the other end, "do you think they'll believe you simply found it there?"

"Who is this?" the D.A. asked.

"Do you think your colleagues, and, importantly, your constituents, will not have their doubts about you if they find out what you keep on your desktop in your home?"

"*Who is this!*"

"Do you think you would ever again have the trust of the public? Do you not need the trust of the public to be elected to an office such as you now hold? And your wife, of course. She will be disappointed, but she will believe whatever you say to her, I am sure. You will even tell her what I assure you now, those young people in the photographs are all above the age of consent, though, as you've seen, they do not look it at all. Quite a good illusion, I think you would agree. People very much love to believe their own eyes."

The D.A. closed the offensive folder. His eyes, jaded and sleepy, could bear no more. He thought again to dump the folder in the trash, but whoever put it on his computer in the first place could simply replace it. Who, he wondered, what tech could he trust to scrub the computer, possibly over and over again, and not reveal the reason?

And, if this folder had appeared on his computer in relation to the Kennedy problem, how much did his caller know about how much he had already cooperated with Errol Kushner to hamstring the investigation into the Kennedy crimes?

He lifted his tumbler of scotch and drained it.

"What do you want?" he asked.

The water was back on when I got home. The repair had turned out, thankfully, to be a smaller job than Yousef or his plumber had prepared me for.

I dumped the bowls of water I'd drawn and left them to dry at the side of the sink, washed my dinner plate, and then I prepared for bed: the pleasure of a quick shower, the routine of a thorough scrub of the teeth in the sink, the lovely flush of a working toilet. It was always the small things – running water – that made life seem manageable.

I went to the kitchen area of my apartment and poured myself a glass of water from the tap. I'd had a great deal to drink that day; staying hydrated would circumvent a hangover.

I changed into a pair of gray sweatpants and a fleece pullover – they would serve for pajamas on this cold, Moroccan night – and hurried through the chill to retrieve my book from the balcony. I arranged myself with Stieg Larsson in the colorful covers and pillows of my single bed – forty pages left until then end, enough to keep my brain occupied so I wouldn't think of Merida, of David and Candace and Jack Cohen, until I fell asleep with the book in my lap. I wouldn't sleep soundly, of course – there was always the possibility of footsteps on my staircase, a rap at my door, the invasive thoughts of people and places I might never see again…

Such is the life of the fugitive. I sighed. Always waiting for the next surprise.

Get the Water Street Crime Starter Library FOR FREE

Get four, full-length ebooks – **BLOODY PARADISE, FROM ICE TO ASHES, TROPICAL ICE,** and **SING FOR THE DEAD** – and lots more exclusive content, all for free!

Building a relationship with our readers is the very best thing about publishing. We occasionally send newsletters with details on new releases, special offers and other bits of news relating to Water Street Press.

And if you sign up to the mailing list we'll send you all this free stuff:

1. A free ebook edition of the exotic thriller **BLOODY PARADISE** – "…a spicy thriller…"
2. A free ebook edition of the crime thriller **FROM ICE TO ASHES** – "designed to shoot the ice down your spine…"
3. A free ebook edition of the eco-thriller **TROPICAL ICE** – "…well-spun, tautly written…"
4. A free ebook edition of the delightfully noir-ish mystery **SING FOR THE DEAD** – Foreword Reviews' Gold Medal winner
5. Advance notice about the release of new Water Street Crime novels.

You can get all this and more, for free, just by signing up at
**https://mailchi.mp/waterstreetpressbooks.com/
waterstreetcrimemailinglist**

Did you enjoy this book? You can make a big difference for our amazing Water Street Crime authors.

Reviews are the most powerful tools in our arsenal when it comes to getting attention for our books. Much as we'd like to, we don't have the financial muscle of a New York publisher. We can't take out full-page ads in the newspaper or put posters on the subway.

(Not yet, anyway.)

But we do have something much more powerful and effective than that, and it's something that those publishers would kill to get their hands on.

A committed and loyal bunch of readers.

Honest reviews of our books help bring them to the attention of other readers.

If you've enjoyed this book we would be very grateful if you could spend just five minutes on Amazon or the online vendor of your choice leaving a review (it can be as short as you like).

Thank you very much.

ABOUT THE AUTHOR

Joe Calderwood is the author of the Clint Kennedy Crime Series, which includes the novels, *Stained Fortune, Money Faucet,* and *Hard Cash,* and the short story collection, *The Dance of Death.* He was born and raised in Homestead, Florida and graduated from college in 1971 with a BBA. For many years he was a practicing CPA in Florida before beginning his career as a serial entrepreneur. He's owned, so far, seven different businesses, currently a fifty-five lot development in Western North Carolina. He lives in Western North Carolina with his spouse of three years – though the two have lived together thirty-six years, only recently the Supreme Court allowed them to marry.

ALSO FROM WATER STREET PRESS

Ready for more thrills?

We suggest The Grand, by Dennis D. Wilson, the first
in his Dean Wister Crime Series.

Have you read all the books in the Water Street Crime
collection? Check out Water Street Press at this link and
see all the amazing books we have to offer:
https://www.waterstreetpressbooks.com

JOE CALDERWOOD

STAINED
FORTUNE

"...GREED, MONEY, DRUGS... AN ENGROSSING THRILLER..."

Enjoy this excerpt from
STAINED FORTUNE,
the first book in the Clint Kennedy Series
by Joe Calderwood.

1

had not planned on ending up back in jail. But when the rewards are great, the risks are often greater.

I remembered how it felt the first time I'd entered jail, the edge of fear that seemed to jab at my nerve endings like the tip of a knife – a sensation I did not find completely unpleasant. Ambition had landed me here, certainly, but I couldn't discount that the nearly carnal satisfaction of an adrenaline rush didn't have something to do with how high I was willing to aim, or how far I'd go to meet my goals.

The other inmates – six in the cell of the Mexican jail I was led to – were hard-pressed to contain their desire to pounce on me as I took my seat among them on the cold, damp concrete floor. Child molesters, rapists, robbers, murderers, assorted minor scam artists – my new compatriots, their hair gelled to porcupine points at the top of their heads, dusty feet in battered flip-flops, dark and shining eyes assessing me.

The prison housed hundreds in cramped cells like this, dungeons with a toilet as the feature at the center of the room, a dank, brown liquid coagulated at its base and a metal seat for seven or more prisoners to use – no privacy and no toilet paper. Weeds sprouted from the cracks in the concrete floor, and the small, damp room smelled of body odor and spent bodily fluids. It was clear the toilet didn't get a lot of use; the inmates pissed wherever they stood.

Pedro, Luis, Gustavo, Manuel, Jose, Carlos – I was the only one with white skin among the mix of Spanish, Mayan, and Mexican prisoners. Most spoke Spanish, or Mayan, with only a spattering of English among them, but I spoke enough Spanish to make myself understood, and to understand that their conversation was about me, and irreverent.

Fortunately for me, Mexico – unlike America in these early years of the new century – was still an aspirational country. My new prison friends appreciated American men like me: they didn't resent my fresh, new, costly clothes or my expensive haircut; they enjoyed the appearance of money, and their proximity to someone who looked like he had a lot of it.

2

The intent to make my fortune was what had landed me in jail the first time, but make my fortune I had, in spite of the temporary obstacle of incarceration. At just thirty-four, and with a fat bank account, I'd moved to Mérida, in the Yucatan, "The White City" named for the common color of its old buildings, and for its cleanliness. I'd bought and restored an eight- bedroom colonial mansion for my home. I spent my days drinking beer by my pool, reading a book or watching an old movie on TV, and feasting on the local dishes my houseboy, Pedro, prepared for me – *Poc Chuc* and *Papadzules*. My nights were spent drinking Scotch and making the rounds of restaurants, art galleries and the symphony that made up the vibrant cultural life of the city. The Mérida population includes the largest percentile of indigenous persons in Mexico – Mayans, most of whom were still struggling to reach even the lowest rung of the ladder their Mexican neighbors sat upon – and so I took it into my head that I would help them in their rise, though perhaps in an even more practical way than I'd been helped in mine: I'd bought three additional old colonials, each smaller than my residence, though just a few streets away, and was in the process of combining them into one building and restoring it as a school for Mayan kids. It was a deeply and not surprisingly satisfying way to spend my time, and my money.

Taavi, for one, wouldn't have been surprised. Maybe he was the one who put the idea in my head in the first place – roused himself from eternal sleep and whispered it to me in my dreams. That would have been something he would have done, if at all possible, and who was to say it wasn't?

In any case, my life was paradise, and it wasn't enough.

Who's to say what's "enough"? What is plenty for one man is paltry to another. I had wads of dollars in my pocket and stacks in my safe and rows and rows of numbers on my balance sheets, but when it came to thrills, I was poverty-stricken.

About three months after my move to Mexico, in the early spring of 2008, I volunteered as a worker for the Yucatan elections – the one hundred and six "municipal presidents", or mayors as we call them in the U.S., that were to be elected that May. Those few weeks of volunteer work consisted mostly of answering phones in various campaign headquarters, posting yard signs where they were permitted – and sometimes where they were not permitted, approaching area business people with a fundraising pitch on behalf of the resident power brokers and decision makers. You could call me a "people person". From the time I was a kid, I could always pick out the ones who would be most beneficial to know. I worked my ass off for the local pols and, by the time the elections were over, I had a whole new group of friends. Politics is an inherently dirty business and the pollution among the Mexican political class is deservedly legendary; I figured someone in that crowd could get me into a little bit of much-needed trouble.

3

My trouble came with a name: Alvaro.

I met Alvaro – met him *formally* – at the victory party for the candidate in Mérida's Third District. He – Alvaro, not the candidate; the candidate was a forgettable little puke who would later be indicted for removing his opponent's advertising materials and exchanging cash for voting cards – was a solid six feet tall, with a body of lean muscle and a head of wavy, thick black hair. Even at first glance he seemed too lithe and graceful – too *physical* – to be a politician. Periodically he'd throw an arm around the smaller but exceptionally beautiful man at his side; the way he looked down at his companion, the smile he gave him, made me wonder if they were a couple. Both of them were surrounded by the circle of spectators who'd gathered around Alvaro, a crowd of men and women who looked up at Alvaro less as just another guest at the victory party but as if they were his fans. There were a few people among that crowd who looked too alert and wary to be simply guests; they looked like Secret Service guys if Secret Service guys routinely dressed in Irish linen guayaberas.

"Do you know who that is?"

"What?" I turned to the Mayan who'd been on the candidate's PR team. I didn't catch his name, but he looked enough like Taavi to draw me to him when I'd first arrived at the party and he'd taken it upon himself to give me the lay of the land – point out the important people I might like to know.

He gestured now toward Alvaro with the hand that held his frothy cocktail. "You think you recognize him, don't you? He's Alvaro Moreno, the bullfighter – not as well-known as his brother, Oscar, but Alvaro's the one who stabbed and killed the Intimidator."

I nodded. "I've never been to a bullfight in my life."

4

"Politicians and bullfighters, there is no difference between them," Alvaro told the crowd. "If you are a bullfighter, the bull is your opponent. He is the one you are trying to beat in the race, the one you do not want to lose the election to, hmmm?" he continued, and the people around him chuckled. "And everything a bull-fighter does, every move he makes, is to do one of three things – distract his opponent, so the opponent is confused and can't fight back as well; anger his opponent, so the opponent makes a stupid mistake; cause injury to his opponent, so the spectators will see the bullfighter is strong and his opponent, this massive animal, is weak." By the time he finished, the people around him were laughing in earnest. He didn't need to twist to one side as if to dodge attack, his hands holding an imaginary cape, to keep his audience captive; that flourish at the end was all showmanship.

But when he'd twisted he'd ended up directly in front of me.

I stretched my hand out to him. "I'm Clint Kennedy. New to the area –"

Alvaro put up a hand and let his black eyes wander over my white skin, blonde hair, blue eyes. "New to the area? Who would have guessed such a thing?" he asked, sending the people who were still gathered around him into another gale of laughter.

I might have been put off – distracted – by his greeting, but that was just what he wanted.

"I've never been to a bullfight. I'd love to see you in the ring."

"You would?" he laughed, and he grabbed the beautiful man who'd been standing near to him and kissed him on the neck. "Then what do you say, Javier? I fight again in, what is it? Two weeks? Should we invite this Mister Clint Kennedy to be our guest?"

Javier shrugged, but he smiled as well. "I think Mister Clint Kennedy would like that, Alvaro."

"Then that's what we will do!" Alvaro boomed. He reached out at last to take the hand I had offered him. "Pleased to meet you, Clint. Call me Alvaro – and this is Javier, my brother-in-law."

Brother-in-law, I thought as I began to loosen my hand from Alvaro's grip in order to shake hands with Javier. *This relationship might be more complicated than I assumed…*

But I didn't get to either finish the thought or offer Javier my hand. Alvaro kept his fist tight over mine and yanked me toward him to whisper in my ear, "I know who you are, Mister Clint Kennedy."

www.ingramcontent.com/pod-product-compliance
Lightning Source LLC
Chambersburg PA
CBHW020658180626
46816CB00003B/1338